MADE MEN V

ANGEL

SARAH BRIANNE

YOUNG INK PRESS

Young Ink Press Publication
YoungInkPress.com

Connect with Sarah:
AuthorSarahBrianne@gmail.com
www.facebook.com/AuthorSarahBrianne
@AuthorSarahBri

ANGEL

THE FALLEN ANGEL

Oh, shit. Oh, shit. Oh, shit.

There was a slight pep in her step as she got off the elevator and headed toward his office. To say she was head over heels and completely and utterly obsessed with the man she was going to see would be an understatement.

Stop it. He's with Chloe now.

She stopped in her tracks, the pep in her step suddenly vanishing.

Lucca was with Chloe now, and though she was in love with the dark demon, he didn't look at her the way he looked at his scarred beauty. In fact, he never had, and she doubted he had ever even seen the way she looked at him.

They're perfect for each other 'cause ... With a longing sigh, she quietly admitted to the universe what she hadn't been able to before, "They're soulmates."

Since finding out Lucca and Chloe were officially a "thing," she hadn't been able to look at Lucca the same, knowing she wasn't meant for him. Now, all she could hope for was to find a man who was made for her, a man who could make her forget all about Lucca, a man who could make her forget about the boogieman.

Pft. Yeah, good freaking luck with that.

Resuming her steps toward his office, the excitement gone, she told herself she would now and always at least enjoy the opportunity of being in his presence … and the view.

Others might fear being called into the boogieman's office for the first time, but not her. It only enticed her. The dark, dangerous part of him was what drew her in more and more each day.

Seeing that his office door was open, she stepped right up to the doorway with a bright smile. "Hey, Lucca, you wanted to see …" Her voice trailed off when she noticed he was already talking to someone. "Sorry, I didn't notice you were …" Her voice trailed off once more, but this time, it was because her breath had been taken away by the unknown man sitting in front of Lucca as he turned his head toward her.

Holy shit, he's hot.

Her eyes couldn't move from his dark orbs. They were black yet seemed like a light shone from behind them, turning them into a strange shade of dark gray. Drifting her eyes lower, she noticed a tattoo under his left eye, high on his cheek, consisting of four little dots that formed a diamond. When she slowly drifted her eyes farther down, she saw that his neck was completely covered in obscure tats as well. He was unlike anyone she had ever seen, too used to the well-groomed men who made up the Caruso mafia family. One thing was for sure. *He sure as hell isn't a Caruso.*

Lucca's dark voice echoed through the room with a hint of a smile in his words. "I'll be with you in a moment."

She hadn't even realized she was holding her breath until she backed out of the doorway and turned around, walking to a seat outside the door.

Licking her now very dry lips, she couldn't help turning her head back toward the door, hoping for a glimpse of the unknown man. She could hear Lucca's muffled voice as he talked to the man who sat there without expression.

He had dark brown hair that was cut close to the skin on the sides, with longer hair that was pushed back on top, and a short, scruffy beard to match his bad boy aura.

Oh God, stop looking at him.

She quickly snapped her head forward, knowing he was nothing but bad news for her. No way in hell would her family let her get within a five-foot radius of him. Hell, her brother was probably on his way here right now—she swore he had a radar that told him every time she looked at an attractive man. She didn't blame him. The ones she was attracted to were all mostly psychopaths.

She couldn't help turning her head to look at him again, seeing that his tattoos got lost under his dingy dark clothing, only to reappear to completely cover his hands.

Yep, he's a psychopath. The pain this man must have endured to cover the little bit of skin she could see made him one.

Clenching her hands together, she closed her eyes tightly and began to pray. *Please, Lord, help me not fall into the Devil's trap.*

"What are you doing?" Lucca's voice broke her feverous praying.

"I was ..." She quickly stood up to face the gorgeous demon, only to look behind him to see the tatted man picking up a gold ring off Lucca's desk.

As he started to slide it into his pocket, his dark gray eyes turned to see her cholate ones watching him. Finally, an expression passed his face, but it wasn't the *oh-shit-you-caught-me* one you would think he would give her. Instead, as he finished sliding it into his pocket, it was like his dark eyes dared her to tell on him.

Looking back at Lucca, she opened her mouth, shocking herself at what came out of it next. "N-nothing. I wasn't doing anything."

Going back to his desk, Lucca nodded to the thief. "I'll see you later, Angel."

Angel? Jeez, she *was* in trouble with a man like him who had a name like that.

If he hadn't just stolen something from Lucca fucking Caruso, she might have taken it as a good sign that he wasn't a trap from Satan himself. But since he did have the big-ass balls to steal from the boogieman, it was a sign from God telling her to stay very fucking far away from him, reminding her that Lucifer had been a fallen angel before becoming the king of Hell.

God, protect me from this man, she prayed as he slowly walked toward her like a beautiful, dark angel, his eyes piercing through to her soul.

Her breath caught in her throat again when he lifted his hand, putting a long, tatted finger to his lips, the quietest "Shh" passing them only for her to hear.

Fuck, I'm doomed. No amount of praying was going to save her. God sure as hell wasn't saving her from the fallen angel before her, or from herself.

She turned her head, following him with her eyes as he passed her before disappearing.

She couldn't help feeling a strange sensation, like a piece of herself left with him, and a piece of him stayed with her. As if when he passed her and slightly grazed her arm, he took a piece of her aura, while she took a piece of his. It had taken her breath away and brought it back in a huge wave. Now she was unable to catch it.

Lucca's brow rose, his same dark voice with a smile echoing once more through the dim room, asking, "Adalyn?"

Trying *to shake off the* thought of the man who had just stolen a piece of her, she turned back to Lucca, trying to pull herself together. "Yes, sorry. Um, you wanted to see me?"

Lucca stared at her for a moment, the amused look on his face never wavering. "I did?"

"Yes …?" Adalyn stared back at him in confusion. "You asked me yesterday to come by your office at noon."

"Must have slipped my mind," he said simply as he leaned back in his chair. "I'm taking Chloe out to lunch in thirty minutes, and I have some work to get done before then, so if you don't mind."

Her mouth dropped open, and her brows furrowed, even more confused as she started to head out the door.

"Have a good day, Adalyn." The smile in his voice gave her a bit of a chill.

"Y-you, too."

Walking away from the strange encounter, she wasn't exactly sure what had just happened. *What the heck?*

She began her journey back the way she had come, heading toward the elevator. *Why did he want me here in the first place if he was just going to shoo me awa—*

"Ahh—"

A light scream had started to escape her throat, but it was quickly interrupted by a firm palm covering her mouth while she was pulled into a dimly-lit cleaning closet.

Adalyn looked up at her captor, who was pushing her against the door she had been swiftly pulled through. Staring at the angel before her who held her body spellbound, she could see this was no angel of the light; this angel was of the dark, and his eyes held a promise of wickedness unlike any she had seen before.

"You're not going to scream, are you?" he asked coolly, already removing the tatted hand from her mouth, which indicated his words weren't really a question but an observation.

"How did you know I wouldn't?" Her brow rose. Any other girl he would have pulled into this closet would have in a second.

Angel's dark eyes traveled over her face. "Because you're not scared."

It was true; she wasn't.

She was unable to keep her eyes off the fascinating man. "And how do you know that?"

A smile started to upturn one side of his lips. "You came into Lucca Caruso's office, skipping and smiling, so you're either really fucking stupid or you don't scare easily." With the hand holding her wrist, he began traveling slowly up her arm. "Let's find out, shall we?"

Adalyn stood dangerously still, wondering what he was going to do, until he stopped his hand over her throat, his thumb catching her pulse.

"Strong ... and steady."

It was hard for her not to melt into his light grip. Bad boys were her weakness, and fuck if he didn't seem like the pinnacle of one.

Trying to stay collected being this close to him, she licked her dry lips. "Well, you must not scare easily either, considering you stole from him."

The slight smile on his face seemed to vanish. "I took something that didn't belong to him."

"Does the ring belong to you?"

He reached into his pocket with his free hand and pulled out the gold ring that bore a horseshoe surrounded by diamonds. He stared at it for only a moment before placing it back in his pocket, returning his attention to her. "No, it belongs to a friend." His voice cold and sharp, it was more than obvious he didn't care much for talking.

"Okay, then."

"So, you won't tell?"

"I meant I believe that it actually belongs to your friend"—a smile now came to her lips—"not that I wouldn't tell Lucca."

Maybe I shouldn—

She saw the lightness behind his dark eyes flash as he used the hand on her throat to force her to look up at him even more. At the same time, he moved his face and body ever so close to her, until there was hardly any space left between them. Then he dropped his voice to a dangerously low tone.

"I don't think you see that I'm the one with the upper hand in this situation, sweetness."

Now her heart raced, and she knew very well he could feel it under his grip, but it wasn't from fear. No, it was from what he was doing to her uncontrollable body. It was putty in his hands, and if she didn't get out of here and far away from him soon, the bad boy would find out exactly what kind of upper hand he had with her.

"You're not going to hurt me," she told him with just as much certainty as he had told her she wasn't going to scream the second he pulled his hand away.

Something in him changed again, bringing the half-hearted smile back to one side of his lips. He brought the hand that wasn't over her throat up to her face, running his long, cold, tatted fingers down the side of her cheek to gradually sweep her thick brown hair behind her left ear. He kept pushing until the locks fell behind her left shoulder, exposing her tanned skin. When he then began to lean down, she would have sworn he was going to kiss her exposed shoulder. Instead, he stopped and turned his mouth to her ear, getting so close that, when he spoke, his scruffy beard tickled it. "You sure about that?"

Adalyn bit her lip, trying to fight the warmth that was rising in her belly. She really, *really* needed to get away before she did something she would soon regret … *Most likely regret.*

"You hurt me, and you're dead. Considering you're not a Caruso, you're in enemy territory. You'll be in much bigger trouble hurting one of their women than if you were simply stealing a ring."

Angel backed up only an inch, telling her he knew she was right.

She turned her head slowly, wanting to look into his dark depths once more before she had to leave.

"Don't worry; I'll keep your secret. But you'll owe me."

He spanned his hand along her throat, stretching her neck up farther. "Sweetness, I'm the last person you'd want owing you."

She could hear the hint of a threat in his tone, but it didn't stop her. Too enticed by the angel, she whispered, "Something tells me I do."

"I was wrong about you." Letting his eyes travel all over her, he finally dropped his hand from her throat as he took a step back. "You *are* stupid."

She guessed a part of her should have been hurt by those words, but she couldn't deny the fact that she must have been stupid for not screaming when he had removed his cold hand from her mouth.

When she twisted the doorknob and cracked the door open, the light from the hallway began to illuminate the shadowy man, causing a dim halo to outline his body. She couldn't help smiling as she stepped out and started closing it, causing the halo surrounding him to slowly disappear.

"Probably, but I wasn't the one stupid enough to steal from a Caruso."

NOT EXACTLY A CARUSO

The next day, Adalyn waited in the fall air for her ride to pick her up and take her to the college. It was always a black Escalade, driven by a Caruso goon, holding her best friend, Lake, as well as Elle and Maria. Another Cadillac always followed them, full of other goons who would guard the girls throughout the day.

Ever since a break-in at the casino hotel, the Carusos no longer took chances, especially with their women. She also figured, by the time Chloe attended college with them next semester, there would most likely be two cars carrying Carusos to protect the underboss's girl.

There was definitely a hierarchy of protection between the girls. At the top was Maria Caruso, a.k.a. the mafia princess. Maria was the daughter of the boss and sister to Lucca and Nero. She was to be protected at all costs. Otherwise, you were certain to die a miserable death … if they got to you before you were able to commit suicide out of failure. Next on the list was Elle, being Nero's girlfriend with one bodyguard to protect her. And then there was Adalyn's BFF, Lake, who was the daughter of a soldier and Adalyn's stepbrother, Vincent's, girlfriend, who happened to be the consigliere's son. Now, since she and Lake shared all the same classes, they happened to also share a bodyguard. However, she knew the bodyguard was there to protect Lake more so than her. And that was where Adalyn's name fell on the list—dead last.

Admittedly, it stung a little bit, because she was utterly fascinated with the family and no part of it frightened her. The family actually intrigued her, making her wish she could become an even more important part of it. It was probably why she had always been in love with Lucca, the underboss and future boss of the mafia family. To be the boss's wife … well, that was as far a woman in the family could get, and Adalyn would have loved every moment of it. Now, there was only one thing she had to have in her future husband … *He has to be Made.*

When a black car pulled up instead of the usual Escalade, she grew worried, wondering if something had happened. She quickly went up to the driver's side to see her and Lake's usual bodyguard, Tom.

"Is everything okay?" she asked, just as her eyes travelled to the man sitting in the passenger seat. Trying to stay cool, she could tell the tatted bad boy hadn't been expecting her either.

"Yes, everything's fine," Tom soothed her fears. "This is Angel. He's going to be helping me watch you girls at school from now on."

"Hi." Adalyn smiled like he hadn't just pulled her into a cleaning closet yesterday.

Angel gave her a quick nod before turning his head forward.

"Where's the Escalade?" she asked, desperately wanting to talk to Lake.

"It's not coming. Get in."

Um, okay . . .?

Going to the back door, she slid in. Sitting behind Tom, she had the perfect side view of the dark Angel.

So, does this mean he is *a Caruso? He doesn't look like one . . .* She couldn't help noticing the tats, the beard, the lack of a suit. *Plus, what Caruso in their right mind would steal from Lucca?*

The thoughts swirled in her head as the car travelled through the city, until her curiosity got the best of her and she could no longer hold it in.

"Are you a Caruso?"

Angel didn't look back, nor did he say anything.

Adalyn then looked at Tom in the rearview mirror. "Is he?"

When Tom looked at her through the mirror, it was obvious he wasn't sure how to respond. "Not exactly."

One of her eyebrows rose. "Then how does a 'not exactly a Caruso' get the job of watching Caruso girls?"

"By Lucca giving him the job," he told her matter-of-factly.

"So, he's trying to become Made," she whispered under her breath, smiling.

"I said, he's not *exactly* a Caruso, not that he wasn—" That was all Tom got out before Angel's low voice spoke over him.

"We don't tell our women about our family business, especially not the little girls."

Adalyn's face dropped as she crossed her arms in front of her chest. *"Excuse me?* I am *not* a little girl."

Again, Angel didn't reply to her retort, which was starting to rub her the wrong way.

Smiling, she began to quietly mutter under her breath, "I don't think you thought of me as a little girl yesterday in the clo—"

"What do you do when they don't listen to you?" Angel had turned his head to look at Tom.

Tom looked confused. "The girls?"

"Yes. How do you reprimand them?"

Clearing his throat, a serious look came over the driver. "We don't punish our women, if that's what you're asking. And you are most certainly never to touch one of them."

Welp, too late for that.

"Okay, but that doesn't answer my question of what you do when they don't listen to you."

"Only two of them seem to like to cause trouble from time to time, and I'll take care of them if they give you any."

Angel gave a quick nod before asking one more question. "Who are the two who cause trouble?"

"Maria is a real pain in the ass, but ..." Tom paused, looking in the rearview mirror at a smug Adalyn. "That one in the back, you have to be careful of. She tends to do things without thinking them through carefully."

"You don't say?" Angel's voice held a hint of sarcasm.

THE SPAWN OF SATAN

Getting out of the car, she felt relief. To say it was a strange car ride would be an understatement. The awkwardness between Angel and her was very apparent, and she could only hope Tom hadn't noticed. Actually, it should be the thieving Angel who should pray Tom hadn't—it was going to be his funeral.

As Adalyn walked up to the girls who stood beside the Escalade and their bodyguards, waiting for her to reach them, she couldn't help noticing that Lake's and Elle's eyes had grown round, admiring the new eye candy. Meanwhile, Angel had the opposite effect on Maria, a hard look crossing her soft features as she crossed her arms.

Adalyn found herself somewhere between the girls on the spectrum of liking Angel—yes, she couldn't deny how hot the bad boy looked, but damn if he hadn't pissed her off by ignoring her in front of Tom because she was a "little girl."

Maria looked the tatted newcomer up and down. "Why is *he* here?"

I guess she knows exactly who he is, which was good considering she still had no freaking clue.

"Because your brother gave him this job," Tom answered.

"You're kidding?" Maria laughed before she pulled her phone from her Louis Vuitton bag and dialed a number before putting it to her ear. "Why the hell is—" was all she got out before she went silent, listening to the other end of the call for several moments. By the time she ended the call, her face had gone from quickly thinking it was a joke to the hard expression she had worn when she had seen him getting out of the car.

An unbothered Angel stood there, uncaring, like she wasn't even talking about him.

The mafia princess wanted to make something clear. "He better not be for me," she told Tom.

"Lucca didn't assign him to you," Tom reassured her.

Flipping her beautiful blonde, long locks behind her shoulder, she walked up to the dangerous-looking man. Her already long legs, made more so by her tall stilettos, made her not much shorter than him.

"I'm not sure what Lucca was thinking assigning you to this job, but we better not have a problem."

Adalyn, Lake, and Elle all looked at each other with *oh-shit* faces.

His dark gray eyes bore into the blonde who had threatened him. "Let's hope not, princess," he said, showing he knew exactly who she was, too.

"Um ... Are we missing something here?" Adalyn could no

longer stand not knowing what the fucking hell was going on.

"He's a Luciano." Maria stepped back, practically spitting out the last of her words at his feet. "But not just any Luciano. He's Lucifer's son."

Oh fuck.

"I would like to go to class now," Elle said before walking off with a Caruso following right behind her.

It was obvious to the rest of them why she had to leave. Elle had protected her best friend, Chloe, all through high school after her friend had been kidnapped and scarred by the one they called Lucifer.

Lucifer Luciano was the mob boss of the Luciano family … until recently, when Lucca removed him from not only the family but this earth. At least, Adalyn was pretty sure Lucca had gutted him after he'd kidnapped Chloe once more, wanting to finish what he had started years ago. Except this time, it was from the Caruso family home.

"Don't ever go near Elle or speak to her," Maria threatened him. "She's the only person Chloe told what happened to her years ago, and they've been best friends ever since."

This time, Angel nodded his head in understanding.

For the first time, Adalyn saw something different behind his gray eyes. What it was exactly, she didn't know.

"Okay, I think it's time you all get to class," Tom interrupted.

Maria walked past Angel, being sure to knock into his shoulder.

Staring at Angel … Luciano, everything that happened between him and Adalyn became a different story. It was a Luciano who had stolen from Lucca. A Luciano who had pulled her into the closet and, like Maria said, *not just any Luciano. He's Lucifer's son.*

A chill went up her spine at the realization that the thing that had been nagging at the back of her mind since she had met him was correct. Angel *did* come from the fucking Devil himself.

He is the spawn of Satan.

Thank God, was all Adalyn could think when they took their seats at the very back of the jam-packed class while Tom and Angel waited outside the door. Their seats sat very close together thankfully, so they could whisper to one another without disturbing anyone. At least, they hoped.

Adalyn pulled her friend in closer to her. Finding out who Angel was changed things, and she was going to definitely need help in the future. "I have to tell you something, and you have to promise to keep it a secret."

"Does it have anything to do with Angel?" Lake asked, knowing her all too well.

"Um . . ."

"Adalyn!" Lake whispered harshly. "I can't promise to keep something away from Vincent if it involves Lucifer's son!"

Stunned, she stared at her best friend since forever. "So, you're picking my brother over *me?* I thought it was hoes before bros?"

"Will you stop pulling that card? You used that on me last week when you wanted McDonalds at one a.m., and I told you I couldn't just 'steal' Vincent's car while he was sleeping to come pick you up to get you some damn chicken nuggets."

"Yes, and I'll never forgive you for that," she huffed, crossing her arms.

"Oh, my gosh … You know you could have just taken yourself, right?"

"No, because then I would have been a shameful fat-ass who needed McDonalds at one in the morning. Everyone knows that if you go with a friend in the middle of the night, it's considered 'cool.' It's like an unspoken rule."

"What kind of rule is this? You're not even fat!" Lake's voice had risen, causing a few students to turn around and look back at them.

Smiling at the lookers, Adalyn waited until they turned their heads back to minding their own business before she turned hers back to her friend. "It doesn't matter if you're physically fat or not; you're just automatically fat if you have to have chicken nuggets in the middle of the night. The rule is real. Ask Maria if you don't believe me."

Lake just stared at her, blinking for a minute, trying to digest the shit Adalyn had just spewed.

"Okay, let's just get back to the topic. Can you keep your best friend's secret? The one who was there for you *way* before your boyfriend ever was?" Adalyn's eyes bore into Lake's, ready to judge her if she said no.

"All right, fine, I promise to keep your secret. But this better not get me in trouble with Vincent."

"It won't if you don't tell him," Adalyn assured her before leaning in closer to whisper softly, "I actually met him yesterday. He may or may not have pulled me into a closet at the casino hotel—"

"He did *what?*"

Adalyn bit her lip, wishing she could have thought this through. "He, you know ... pulled me into a closet."

"Why did he do that? Did he hurt you?" Lake began to really worry.

Adalyn was going to have to be careful since she did want to keep the secret of him stealing the ring from Lucca. "No, he didn't hurt me. He just wanted to talk."

"You don't pull someone into a closet just to talk."

It was really hard to lie to her BFF, but ... *LIE.*

"Well, he did."

"Okay, then, what did he want to talk about?" Lake clearly wasn't buying it.

"He just wanted to get to know me, I gues—"

"Really, Adalyn? You expect me to believe that? Why tell me this secret if you're not going to really tell me?"

"Because ..." She paused, taking a deep breath, wondering if she should reveal this part. "I need you to keep me away from him. He's bad news, and I know it. But ... you know how I get when they're hot, bad, and hot."

"You said he was hot twice ... Oh God, you like him." Lake's wariness was only getting worse.

"No, I don't. I said I think he's hot, not that I like him. I actually think he's a sexist jerk, and I don't know why I find him attractive, anyway."

"Oh, no. Oh, no. Oh, no."

"What? Are you okay?" Adalyn was beginning to worry something was wrong with Lake.

"That's how Elle felt with Nero, how I felt with Vincent, and how Chloe felt with Lucca. You see where I'm getting at?"

She gulped loudly, and the hairs on the back of her arms stood up. "Oh, no."

"He's Lucifer's son ... a Luciano ... and you're a Caruso," she whispered. "God help you."

A story had been told for Elle, Lake, and Chloe, and now it was like she could feel the book of the rest of her life opening, but it didn't have her name on it.

It held the name: *Angel.*

The question was: did she want to jump in it? If she did, it was almost inevitable they would crash and burn due to his last name. The families hadn't mixed blood as far as she knew ... *ever.*

A NICE NAME...
FOR AN UNFORTUNATE GIRL

hifting his weight to his right foot after standing there for so long, he checked his watch to see how much longer he had to endure this torture. *Fuck, this is boring.*

A buzzing noise had him reaching for his phone in the back pocket of his jeans.

"Do you mind?" he asked the man beside him, who had been watching him like a hawk all day. Tom was supposed to be showing him the ropes, and even though the Caruso was trying his best to hide the fact that he was watching his every move, it was obvious to a man like Angel.

"Sure." Tom nodded, giving him the go-ahead.

Walking a bit of distance away to keep his conversation private, he answered the phone with a "Yes?"

"How is it?" a voice similar to his asked.

"Slow."

"I wouldn't say that. You're at a college, surrounded by hot girls. You were always the lucky bastard between us."

Angel's voice went low. "You mean lucky enough to be the one chosen?"

"Yeah, well, there is no fooling Lucca Caruso. Your name might be Angel, and out of the two of us, others might think you are one, but we both know you're the evil twin."

Angel smiled, knowing his twin brother Matthias was right. They'd had their fun ever since they were born, letting everyone think Matthias was the strongest, smartest, and meanest one, but in reality, it was him.

Growing up the way they did, it wasn't easy, to say the least, so making everyone think they shouldn't mess with Matthias while they always ignored or underestimated Angel had protected them. It was their armor. Over the span of their lives, very few had found out the truth about them, and when they had, they'd realized too late.

Until Lucca.

"Did you get it yet?" Matthias asked, getting to the real reason of the phone call.

Feeling the heavy weight of the ring deep in his pocket, he was able to tell him what he had been unable to yesterday. "I did."

"Then it must have gone successfully."

"Well, not exactly." The image of the troublesome little brunette filled his mind. "I didn't realize I had an audience."

"Who?" A hint of worry appeared in Matthias's voice.

"A Caruso girl."

The wariness in his brother's voice turned dark. "Will she be a problem?"

"I'll take care of her," he put simply, without a hint of remorse.

"Good." Matthias paused. Knowing Angel would do whatever it took, he then gave his brother a final warning with the dark tone still present, "Be careful, Angel. Remember, no matter how much time you spend with them, you are and always will be a Luciano, never a Caruso."

Angel looked at Tom, who remained down the hall, as he put his hand deep in his pocket. Seeing Tom's muscles tighten and his eyes slightly narrow, becoming trained on what Angel was about to pull out of his pocket, revealed to Angel all he needed to know.

Rubbing his thumb over the ring, he thought about who it belonged to and why he had stolen it back. *For family.*

"I know, brother," was all he said before he hung up and headed back to the spot he had come from.

When he finally pulled his hand out of his pocket, coming up clean, he saw Tom ease again. He had to refrain from rolling his eyes to the back of his head. *Stupid fucker.*

No, there was no fooling Angel, who knew every trick in the book when it came to watching someone. He had become an expert at it, and had gone undetected due to the act he played. Not only that, but the reason he had learned how to have a watchful eye in the first place was because he had felt what it was like to be watched from a very young age. Feeling the judgmental eyes of others was something he could and always would feel. It never failed to make his skin crawl …

…"You can each pick one thing," his older brother, Dominic, had told them when they'd walked into the busy gas station.

Angel couldn't help noticing the stares they got the second they walked in; not only from the customers, but the cashier, too. He wasn't sure why they were looking at them that way. He wondered if it was because of the dirty, dingy clothes they wore, or if it was because their thirteen-year-old brother was taking care of his eight-year-old twin brothers.

"Ooo … I want this." Matthias grabbed a bag of gummies from off the shelf.

"No." Their older brother snatched the gummies out of his hand, putting it back. "It's breakfast; pick doughnuts or something. Just hurry up or we're going to be even later for school."

It was hard for Angel to concentrate on picking something when the cashier came out from behind the counter to watch them closer. Therefore, he just grabbed a pack of powdered doughnuts, not wanting to make his brother any later.

Dominic took them to their elementary school every morning before he went to his classes at the middle school, which always caused him to be late. The school was going to fail his older brother if he continued with his tardiness.

"You better be paying for those, boy, and I want to check all your backpacks before you leave. You little shits are sneaky nowadays," the foul-looking cashier spat at Dominic.

Now Angel understood why everyone was staring at them.

Looking down at his dirty clothes, he figured it didn't look like they had enough *money to afford a pack of gum.*

"We have money," a young Dominic growled back as he picked up a honey bun for himself.

The cashier laughed in their faces. "Yeah, I bet you do."

A flash appeared behind his brother's eyes. Even though he was only thirteen, his height and stature made him look older.

Taking a step toward the man, Dominic growled once more, pulling out a twenty-dollar bill their father had thrown at them earlier, "I. Said. We. Got. Money."

Sure, they weren't rich, but money was never the issue. With their father being who he was, people would give him their life savings if they thought he wanted it badly enough. The issue was parenting.

Turning his back to them, the cashier headed toward his spot behind the register. "Good, then pay for your shit and get outta here."

"Do you know who our father is?" Dominic asked so coldly that the obese man stopped in his tracks. Then a simple whisper revealed a name that had the customers scurrying to leave. "Lucifer."

The eyes that had stared at Angel in suspicion now held fear. In that moment, he would never forget how it felt like thousands of dung beetles covered his body as their tiny legs skated across his skin.

The old man began to stutter, about to piss himself. "I-I-I didn't know. I-I'm s-sorry."

"Matthias, get the candy you wanted," Dominic ordered his little brother without taking his eyes off the cashier.

Matthias wasted no time obeying, grabbing the gummies he had originally picked up and holding them with his second choice of plain doughnuts.

Putting the twenty back in his pocket, Dominic grinned as they all began to leave. *"If you'd like, I'll have my dad come by to pay you back?"*

All the cashier did was violently shake his head from side to side.

"Thought so." Dominic spat on the floor before leaving.

It was everything Angel could do not to run from the eyes and the whispers that had travelled through the air, but he hadn't. Instead, he had chosen to walk steadily beside his proud older brother while making a silent promise to himself that he would do whatever it took not to have the beetles crawl over his skin again . . .

. . . The doors he stood beside flew open as students started to file out. He waited until it seemed like no one was left when the door flew open again, two giggling girls coming out. The tall brunette already belonged to a Caruso, but the short one was the one who had already gotten under his skin.

Following behind them with Tom, he whispered over to him, "Exactly who did Lucca assign me to watch?"

When his question was answered with a single smile, Angel's eyes went back to the short, troublesome brunette.

Adalyn.

It was a nice name . . . for an unfortunate girl.

CHICKEN NUGGETS
WAIT FOR NO ONE

Monday, *Wednesday, and Friday were* the girls' long days, having two classes in the morning and one in the afternoon, giving them time for lunch in between. They usually went to the cafeteria during their break, which gave them a couple of options, or one of the few fast food options in the school's mini food court—Adalyn's obvious favorite.

They also usually met Elle and Maria at the cafeteria, but Adalyn wondered if they might eat off campus today, considering who was just a few feet behind her, following her, distracting the hell out of her.

"You okay?" Lake whispered for her ears alone.

No. "Yes."

Her friend's face didn't look like she had bought the lie.

Reaching the cafeteria, Adalyn was shocked to see the other girls already sitting at a table with their food. By the look on Maria's face, she didn't seem pleased, especially as she watched Angel take a seat at the table next to theirs with the other Carusos.

Honestly, Adalyn's face didn't look happy either, but hers was because of the food on Elle's plate, which consisted of beef tips in some gross-looking brown gravy, and Maria's plate, which was the same every day—some leaves from the salad bar. *Ew.*

"That looks good, Elle. I think I'm gonna get that." Lake eyed her plate.

Adalyn practically choked on the bile coming up from her stomach. "The hell it does!"

"I think it tastes pretty good," Elle said, taking a bite.

Even Maria made a disgusted face at her. "That's why I got a salad."

Rolling their eyes, they all snapped at the beautiful blonde who cared about her appearance a little too much, "You always get a salad!"

"You're really gonna eat that gross stuff that looks like it cost them five cents to make?" Adalyn looked at her BFF, praying she said *no.*

"I grew up on poor people food, remember? I was raised to never turn down good-looking, cheap food. You two will never understand." Lake looked back at her friend and Maria, knowing Elle had grown up frugal, too.

"You're nasty, and I can't believe you're gonna make me eat leaves instead of going to the food court."

"I'll take you," a laidback voice spoke, making them all turn their heads to see Angel appearing as laidback as his voice.

"Really?" she asked, contemplating it, even though that meant she would be alone with him. She then looked toward Tom to see if he would even allow it and was answered with a nod.

Hm, I don't know if I should . . .

Maria flipped her hair. "Salads taste goo—"

"Let's go." Adalyn quickly stood, cutting off her nonsense and hurting the blonde's feelings, *if she even has any.*

"This is to pay for her food." Tom handed a platinum card to Angel.

Adalyn was already halfway to the food court before he placed the card in his pocket. *Chicken nuggets wait for no one.*

"I'll take the twenty-piece nuggets." She smiled at the cashier before turning to look at Angel. "You want anything?"

"Um, no thanks."

While he handed the card over to the cashier, a beautiful bag filled with nuggets was brought to the counter.

"Thank you, God," she said, taking the bag and filling it with ketchup packets before going to a small table.

Angel joined her as she pulled the contents from the bag and began pouring out ketchup to dunk the nuggets in.

Popping one in her mouth, she tried to break the awkwardness between them. "You sure you don't want anything?"

A nod was all she got from the tatted man sitting across from her, leaning back in his chair with his arms crossed in front of him. He looked like he had not a care in the world.

"How's your first day going?" she asked, trying to start another conversation with him.

This time, all she got was a shrug.

Her blood was beginning to boil now. She didn't care for his attitude and wondered if she had a penis, would he talk to her then?

"Are you ever going to say more than two words to me?"

"I said I would take you here, not talk to you," he told her simply.

Smiling big, she couldn't help herself. "And I said I wouldn't tell anyone about your thieving hands, but it just might slip out."

His black depths flashed at her before a long, ink-covered hand reached out toward her. She didn't know what to expect and was shocked when he took a nugget from her pile and dipped it in the ketchup.

"You talk a lot."

She pulled them closer to her. "And you steal a lot."

"You can't really eat all those, can you?" he asked before placing the stolen one in his mouth.

"Watch me."

Going back to his uncaring pose, he was the one to keep the conversation going. "Does Lucca always buy your food?"

It took her a second to realize he must have been referring to Lucca's name being on the card Tom had given him. She thought it was a weird question for him to ask, yet she figured she wasn't telling him anything he wouldn't know soon enough. "He makes sure we're not only safe here at school, but taken care of, too."

The hidden look on his face was telling her he had an opinion on that.

"Something wrong about that?"

Reaching over slower this time, he took another nugget. "I think he babies you girls."

She couldn't be more appalled. "He does not."

"Does, too. I doubt any woman or girl in the Caruso family has a job."

Adalyn had to actually think for a second. "That's not true at all."

"Are they married to soldiers?" he asked, knowing all too well what the answer was.

So what? "The ones who are married to men higher up all have children to take care of—that's a job."

"Yes, it is, but not all mothers have the luxury to get to be stay-at-home moms."

"I know that, but what do you want me to say? Sorry that Lucca and our family are letting us get an education *to work* in the future? It's not like we're being lazy."

Stealing another nugget, he smiled devilishly as he dunked it into the ketchup generously. "No, but you are spoiled."

"Will you stop stealing my freaking nuggets!" She pulled them even closer to her and to the very edge of the table. "And I'm not spoiled! I feel sorry for the women in the Luciano family," she scoffed.

"You shouldn't. We take great care of them." That devilish smile still clung to his lips as he finished with a wink that almost made her forget about his sexist comment.

"I bet you do," she said so sarcastically she hoped he couldn't hear the secreted swoon in her voice. However, she was sure he noticed by the smug look on his face. Instead of mentioning it, though, he said something else as he leaned back.

"Your friends are coming."

"Is Maria with them?" Taking a bite of a nugget, she could only hope.

Crossing his arms over his chest, his face went back to not giving a fuck. "Unfortunately."

She actually chuckled before she remembered she was supposed to hate him. "Thief."

"Brat," he whispered under his breath as he got up to let the girls have the table.

Dammit, Adalyn, get yourself together.

"How were your nuggets?" A suspicious-looking Maria asked as she sat down next to her.

"Amazing."

When Maria went to open her mouth, she stopped her.

"I swear to God, if you say your salad was, too, I'll take your heels off and pull a Maria on yourself."

The pretty blonde snapped her mouth shut.

Elle's big blue eyes became curious. "What's a Mari—"

"Maria," Lake began quickly, knowing the subject needed to be changed, "can you please tell Adalyn that there's no unspoken rule that, if you go to McDonalds at one in the morning, you're automatically considered a fat-ass, no matter your size, but if you go with a friend, it's considered *'cool'*?"

As she reached to steal a juicy nugget, it didn't take her a second to answer, "I can't because it exists."

CHANNING FUCKING TATUM

Walking *through her front door*, she huffed, beginning to mumble underneath her breath, "Stupid jerk. Asshat. Dick—"

"What's wrong with you?"

"N-nothing," she quickly replied, taken off guard. She hadn't seen Vincent sitting on the couch when she had come in.

He suspiciously looked at her for a moment. "You sure about that?"

Remembering how Angel had ignored her completely on the way home, she was about to open her mouth and tell him how much she hated men at the moment, when "Yes" came out instead. Just as well. She would save it until she got *really* pissed off. "Why are you here?"

"Last time I checked, this was still my home."

Throwing herself down on the couch, she sunk into it. "Oh yeah, I forgot you have, like, five homes."

"I have three." Lifting three fingers, he began to list them. "My dad's, my penthouse, and here."

"Aren't you always over at the Caruso house? That's like four."

"We don't really hang out over there much anymore since we got the penthouses. Plus …" Vincent paused for a second. "Lucca may or may not have banned me from the house for the time being."

Busting out in laughter, she could barely get her words out. "He *banned* you? What did you do now?"

"He didn't like the way I smiled at Chloe; said I was flirting with her."

"Were you?" She laughed even harder.

"No! That's just my fucking face!" he yelled over her cackling, getting frustrated.

It was true; it was just his face. Her stepbrother was a pretty boy, born with a gorgeous face. His striking baby blue eyes didn't help either. Flirting came easy to him with the countless girls and women who had thrown themselves at him, and now he didn't even have to try to flirt. It was just … his face. It was like if Jonah Hill smiled at you; it would just be a nice gesture. But if Channing Tatum smiled at you, then … *I don't know about you, but I'm goin' to my grave claiming Channing fucking Tatum flirted with me.*

She was also missing the obvious—him being grossly happy with her best friend. Sometimes she really missed her brother's old, slutty ways when she wanted McDonalds at one in the morning.

"I'm sorry." She tried to contain her laughter. "It must be so hard being beautiful."

Vincent nodded in agreement, clearly not getting her sarcasm. "It's a curse."

"Oh God." Adalyn got up, going to the kitchen. She'd had enough of pretty people shit after Maria earlier today. "At least Maria has a brain," she whispered to herself.

"Did you say something?" Vincent asked, following behind her.

"Nope." Grabbing an apple from the counter, she bit into it while looking at her brother, who looked like he had something to say. "Are you gonna tell me why you're here or not?"

Picking up his own apple, he took a huge bite of what looked like half the apple. "I came to hang out with my favorite sister, is all."

"*Only* sister," she corrected.

"And," Vincent continued, clearly getting to the point, "to see how your day went."

"How my day went?" Staring at him, she quickly realized why he was here. "Does Angel have anything to do with it?"

"Maybe."

"My day was fine. You can leave now. Bye."

"Don't be like that, Adalyn. Lucca's the one who made me ask you. He wanted to make sure you felt comfortable with Angel."

Lucca? "Why wouldn't he just ask me himself?"

Vincent took another bite of the apple, obviously not wanting to answer until she shoved him hard enough. "Probably because he knows you're in love with him."

"I am not!" she lied, of course.

Rolling his eyes, he saw right through her. "Like hell, you're not.

I wouldn't be surprised if him saying *darlin'* is your ringtone and his face is your screensaver."

Excuse me?

Actually, that's not a bad idea . . .

"Don't you have orders you need to go follow or something?"

"Fine." While he threw the core of his apple away, his tone got serious. "For the time being, Angel will be your bodyguard, and even though I don't like it, Lucca insisted. You'll tell me if he does or says anything the family should know, right?"

Gulping down the lump in her throat, she hoped she had somehow become a better liar in the last thirty seconds. "Of course."

His baby blues stared at her a moment longer before he nodded and started to leave, making her sigh in relief. She had seen it in his eyes that he didn't trust Angel for one second.

"Vincent?" she quietly called, making him stop.

Turning around, she now saw hope in his eyes that there was something she knew about Angel that he didn't. "Yes?"

"Do you happen to have a picture of Lucca?"

Angel sat on his bed, rolling the horseshoe ring between his fingers before placing it on his nightstand.

Does the ring belong to you? the brunette's voice rang through his head.

Pulling out his phone, he searched through his contacts, then stared down at the picture that now filled the screen. It was of a slightly younger version of him with his arm wrapped around a beautiful, smiling girl.

Bella.

DEAR HEAVENLY FATHER, IF YOU WANT TO KEEP ME A VIRGIN...

She took a deep breath as the car pulled up. She had decided to start over with Angel and was going to give him a pass for yesterday since it had been his first day on the job. That must have been why he'd treated her that way.

When the car stopped, she slid in, shutting the door behind her, and smiled wide, determined to make this a great day. "Morning, boys."

"Morning," Tom replied, putting the car in drive.

It hadn't been his response she'd been waiting for.

Sitting there patiently, waiting, she realized the tatted one wasn't going to give her a response.

Okay . . .

Adalyn took another deep breath, wanting to try again. "So,

how was your first day, Angel?"

"Fine." It was a quick, almost irritated response.

She couldn't help it when words started spewing from her mouth, uncaring that Tom was there, too. "Do you have a freaking problem with me or something?"

The car fell silent for several moments before his cold, uncaring voice slashed through the air. "Other than you talk too fucking much? Not really."

Stunned, her mouth dropped open. *Asshole.*

Tom laughed. "For once, I think she might be speechless."

"We can only hope," Angel mumbled under his breath, making Tom laugh harder.

Her chocolate depths flashed as she hatefully stared at the *thieving, sexist, piece of shi—*

An evil smile began to finally touch her lips. *I know how to fix this.*

Reaching into her bag, she pulled out her phone and searched through her contacts. Clicking on the name she wanted, she went to send a text message, quickly typing in what she wanted to say. She then wasted no time pressing *Send.*

Adalyn stared down at her phone with a smug look on her face. Reading the name at the top, she finally felt satisfaction. *Lucca.*

Looking back up at Angel, she watched him finally turn his head back to glance at her, seeing a slight bit of concern finally showing through his eyes. It wasn't concern for her, however. It was concern for him. Little did he know that it was too late.

Her eyes travelled back down to the screen, reading the message she had sent.

I need to talk to you about Angel.

Spending the school day with Angel, she couldn't help really concentrating on him. She concluded that she had no fucking clue who he was. He was like an enigma. The more she tried to figure him out, the less sense she made of him.

He should be nice to me, right? I watched him steal the ring . . .

That was the biggest mystery of all. He should *want* to be nice to her to keep her mouth shut, but he was doing the complete opposite, like he was *trying* to piss her off.

She wouldn't understand it next to his careless attitude. He damn sure wasn't much of a bodyguard, considering he was never on alert the way the Carusos were.

A Caruso always stood with his eyes constantly scanning the room, something she never saw Angel do. She wondered if that was the reason for his harsh appearance and tattoos. Maybe he wanted the don't-fuck-with-me look so he didn't have to worry about anyone messing with him. She figured it probably worked, knowing not many people here saw men covered from head to toe in tats.

He was like a rare . . . creature, and there was no way anyone else like him existed.

"Adalyn? Adalyn!" Lake snapped her fingers in front of her face, finally getting her attention.

Adalyn quickly stood, grabbing her things. "Sorry."

"You all right? You're acting kinda weird today."

"Yes. How am I acting weird?" She brushed it off, heading toward the door.

It took Lake a second to figure out what was different about her. "I don't know. You're just awfully quiet, I guess."

"Probably because I was told I talk too effing much by Angel."

"*He did what?* Did Tom hear him say that?" she asked.

"Yep. He laughed." Adalyn went through the open door, halfway hoping it would hit Angel in the face.

"What a dic—" Lake cut herself off when she saw the two bodyguards on the other side of the door.

Rolling her eyes when she saw Angel resting his head against the wall behind him in boredom, Adalyn figured he wouldn't last much longer, so maybe talking to Lucca wasn't necessary anymore.

She continued to walk right past them, starting the journey back to the car since they were leaving their last class of the day.

I bet he's not going to last one more—

A cold hand was wrapped around hers, pulling her backward. It wasn't until Angel's back had somehow managed to end up in front of her did she realize it was his hand.

Angel abruptly thrust his other hand and arm out, stopping the male student who had almost ridden his skateboard right into her.

By the smile the guy on the skateboard had and the laughter from a small group of students who were watching, it became apparent it wouldn't have been an accident if he had collided with her.

Angel twisted his ink-covered fingers into the student's shirt. "You could've fucking killed her."

Adalyn looked down at the hand that had slightly tightened around hers as he'd said those words. A strange feeling washed over her, reminding her of the feeling she had gotten when she had first met him, making her realize that feeling had never left but had just hidden deeper inside her the more he ignored her.

The greasy-haired kid smirked even wider, clearly unaware of the serious shit he had just stepped into. "I had to make sure you goons were doing your job."

As Tom stepped forward, Angel shoved the skater with one powerful move, making him fall to the ground. "Now you fucking do." Then he reached out with his foot, flipping the skateboard up into the air and grabbing it with his free hand.

What the fuc—

Her hand was tugged on to begin walking beside him.

Did that really just happen?

"Hey! That's my board!" the kid still sprawled on the ground yelled behind them.

Okay, it did, but did he just flip it . . . then catch it?

That feeling that was creeping up on her got stronger.

Dammit, stop it! Don't think it!

When he dropped his hand from hers once they left the building, she felt it again—that bizarre sensation that happened when their skins were pulled away from each other's. She felt another piece of her leave with him while she captured another piece of him. It was unlike anything she had felt before, a feeling that should frighten and bring her to her knees in fear of losing herself to him. But it didn't. At least, not yet.

When Angel continued walking, he left her still very much too shocked to move.

Lake stood beside her, apparently just as shocked. "That was, um …"

"Fucking hot," Adalyn finished for her, unable *not* to think it anymore.

They stared as he confidently walked away with the skateboard still in his hand.

"Yep." Lake's voice was a little heavy.

"Do you think he knows how to ride it?" Her voice might have been a little heavy, too.

"We can only pray."

When the two girls began to pray, they prayed for two different things.

Dear Heavenly Father, if you want to keep me a virgin … don't let him ride that damn board.

A BULLET WITH
YOUR NAME ON IT

"**W**here are we going?" *Adalyn* asked when he didn't turn off to head to her house.

Tom looked up in the rearview mirror to look her dead in the eyes. "Lucca asked to see you."

Her eyes grew wide before she quietly nodded. *Oh shit.*

The car ride was silent on the way to the casino hotel, and the walk to Lucca's office was quieter. When they had gotten off the elevator, there was a moment when Angel looked at her, telling her that he knew what she planned to do. His eyes didn't plead with her, however. No, there was something else in them. *Disappointment.*

Knocking on the door, she exhaled, not realizing until then that she had been holding her breath the whole way up.

"Come in."

She walked into the smoke-filled room, taking a seat in front of the beautiful demon. His blue-green eyes practically glowed in the dark room.

Finally, it was his voice to break the silence. "You wanted to talk to me about Angel?"

"Um, yes ..." She cleared her throat, trying to pull her thoughts together. She pictured him taking the ring off Lucca's desk. "He ..." She trailed off, looking down at her hand that had held Angel's.

"He what?" Lucca asked.

It was time for her to make a decision. She only hoped she wouldn't regret it.

Taking a long, deep breath, she made up her mind. "Angel's a dick."

A slow smile appeared. "A dick? How?"

"Yep. And sexist."

"Sexist?" Now he looked a little confused.

Nodding, she continued, "You heard me; he's sexist. He will only talk to the men."

"Well ..." He took a moment, seeming to process this. "He's there to protect you, not talk to you."

"He could at least say good freaking morning."

"Yes, he could." He smiled slightly before it disappeared. "Do you in any way think he's not capable of protecting you?"

"No," she admitted in defeat.

"And is there anything else he has done that could change my opinion of him?"

Her last chance was here. If she was ever going to tell him what Angel did, it would be now. Instead, she whispered the word that would seal her fate. "No."

"Then this is an issue between you and Angel to solve."

She gave a solemn nod as she stood up and headed for the door.

"You sure there's nothing else you wanted to tell me?" His dark voice stopped her as he flicked his lighter, lighting the cigarette he held between his lips.

Does he know?

"Y-yes."

"All right."

Adalyn said a little prayer, thanking God that Lucca didn't know about the ring.

She tried to leave once more, but again he stopped her.

"Room 22008."

What? She looked back at him, confused.

Warm smoke escaped his mouth as he said, "Go talk to him."

She stared at the number 22008 before her, wondering if she really should do it or if this was a test. Her mind was telling her this was a bad idea, whereas her body was already raising her hand to knock on the door.

Did Lucca really say this was okay? Her knuckles meeting the door answered for her.

The longest minute of her life passed before the door was finally swung open to reveal an angel dressed in jeans and a snug black T-shirt that revealed his full-arm tattoo sleeves to her for the first time. It took everything she was to stop looking at the inked skin and to look up at his face.

"H-hi. I was wondering if we could talk."

Not moving from the doorway, Angel pointed up at a camera in the hallway that was focused on his door. "I don't think that would be a good idea."

"Lucca actually told me to come see you."

He stared at her for a few seconds before he finally moved to the side to let her in.

Walking in, she saw the room was just a basic hotel room with a queen bed, a TV, and a little table and chairs. It wasn't on the penthouse floor but the floor below the Caruso residence.

As he closed the door behind him, she grew nervous, never considering she would have gotten this far.

Angel was the one to break the ice as he crossed his tatted arms over his chest.

"So, I guess, since you're here and not Lucca, you decided not to tell him about the ring."

"I don't know wha—"

"Don't fucking lie to me, Adalyn. I'm not stupid," he cut her off coldly.

"Maybe if you weren't such a dick to me, I wouldn't have wanted to tell him," she said matter-of-factly.

As if she wasn't nervous enough, Angel stalked toward her.

"Understand I'm not a nice person, and I treat you no differently than anyone else. Have you even seen me talk to the other Carusos, besides Tom?" He didn't wait for her to respond, knowing the answer already. "I talk to Tom because I have to. So, don't worry, sweetness; you're not special. I don't like anyone."

"Then do yourself a favor and just leave, jerk," she spat.

Having had enough of his attitude already, she headed for the door.

"You misunderstood." Snatching her wrist as she passed, he pulled her back to look up into his dark eyes. "You think I want to fucking be here? I'm being forced to stay here."

"W-what?"

"I'm collateral, sweetness. Lucca's keeping me here to keep peace between the families, to keep the Lucianos in line."

It was all making sense now. She had wondered why the hell he was there after Chloe had been kidnapped by his father. She couldn't help asking the question that now filled the air between them ... "What happens if your family doesn't stay in line?"

"What do you think?" Releasing his tight grip on her wrist, he lifted his hand, making a gun with his fingers, then pointed it to the side of his temple.

Adalyn swallowed down the bile rising in her throat. The look behind his eyes showed her something wasn't quite right about him. He was beginning to let her in; let her see what his eyes truly held.

She backed up slowly, fear settling in, though she didn't know if it was hers or his at this point, but she could see it—see how he felt.

He was trapped. Trapped like an animal.

"You should have told him what I did." He followed her until the back of her legs hit the nightstand and there wasn't an inch of space between them. "Because sooner or later ..."

She closed her eyes when he moved the mock-trigger of the finger gun he held to his skull. It was like the sound of a gun went off in her mind.

Feeling a tap on her head, she opened her eyes again to see his fingers were still in the shape of the gun, but now it was pointed at her. Breathing heavily, she tried to back up again, but the nightstand kept her in place. All she could do was hold on to it to keep her stable.

"Now, if he finds out you know"—he lightly pressed the tip of his inked finger deep into her skin—"there might be a bullet with your name on it, too."

"You're fucked up," she whispered, realizing the depths of which he was.

He moved his cold fingertips down her face until they disappeared to his side. Shutting off his gray eyes to her, they became dead again. "Like father, like son."

"I refuse to believe it."

Angel's jaw flexed. He didn't realize that he had made a mistake. He had let her see the bad, yes. However, he didn't realize she had found the paranoia and behind that, she had found the scars.

"You wouldn't have pushed that guy out of the way today if you were like him. You would have just let him hit me." *That* she truly believed.

Leaning down, he whispered in her ear, giving her a warning he never gave others until it was too late. "Don't underestimate me, Adalyn. It'll be the last thing you do."

Did he just threaten me?

Watching him walk away, she started to move her hands off the nightstand when she felt something metal move against her skin.

"You should leave now."

Adalyn walked to the door he held open, looking into his eyes one last time. She now understood the fallen angel better. She was going to have to be more careful.

Her eyes traveled down to his neck where the black wolf was inked. You could only keep an animal caged for so long before they broke; either giving up to die or going insane trying to become free again.

"Goodbye, Angel."

CHECKMATE, ASSHOLE

Angel sat on the floor, staring at the wooden door that held a metal padlock, knowing it had been quiet for too long.

Getting up, he headed for the living room where he found Dominic cleaning their father's Glocks at the table. Even though Dominic was only thirteen, their father had been teaching him about guns since he was ten. By now, his brother could break down a gun and put it back together in seconds.

Lucifer happened to be sitting next to him at the table, counting money that Angel assumed wasn't his in the first place.

Sitting on the couch, he grabbed the remote and turned on the TV, flipping to a program that he probably shouldn't be watching as gunfire was going off rampantly.

"Turn that shit off, Angel," Lucifer snapped without looking up from the money he was counting.

His little finger hovered over the button for a moment before he pressed it. Then again, and again, and again.

"I said to fucking turn it off!" Lucifer growled as the television's volume was only turned up higher.

He ignored him as he held the remote tightly in his sweaty hands.

With the noise making it impossible to count the money, Lucifer set down the wad of cash before he flew up to stand in front of his son. "Stand up."

Angel looked up at his frightening father, who was seething in anger. He stood up on shaky legs, knowing if he didn't, what was about to come would be much worse.

When the back of a hand met his cheek, it sent his eight-year-old scrawny body flying to the ground. Then everything went blurry as a hand grabbed his wrist and dragged him across the floor. The clicking of metal was all he could hear as Dominic began putting the gun he had been cleaning back together.

He was being pulled down the hallway when he saw his older brother block the view to the living room.

Dominic raised the Glock. Narrowing his eyes, he aimed at the back of their father's head with his finger hoovering over the trigger.

A smile was brought to Angel's lips while he was being dragged across the floor.
Click.

Even though the two brothers knew it wasn't loaded, they both hoped the sound of the gun wasn't one of an empty one. He watched as Dominic disappeared from view as he was dragged into a room, but before he fully disappeared, he saw the visible pride in his older brother's eyes for the very first time.

When his arm was dropped to the floor, he heard a key going into a lock, making him turn his head to see his father slowly opening the padlocked door.

The shaking little body revealed inside the tiny closet started to move when light hit his face. It was like Angel was looking into the very near future of himself when his identical twin brother was pulled from the closet and he was dragged in.

"A-An . . . gel." Matthias tried to speak, but his voice was weak. With horror on his face, he started to realize what Angel had done.

The two had a bond, a connection, so when Angel hadn't heard a noise from the closet in hours, he knew Matthias had been broken. And he had known that if he didn't do something soon, he would have been too far gone.

With the door closing and darkness setting in, Angel could only hope that when the door opened again, he was the same person as when the door closed . . .

. . . Waking up from the nightmare, Angel sat up in bed, his naked body covered in sweat. Turning on the bedside lamp, he ran his hands through his hair, taking long, deep breaths.

It wasn't until a minute later, when his eyes went back to his bedside table, that he realized it was devoid of the horseshoe ring he had stolen.

Getting up, he looked around the floor to see if it had fallen before an image of Adalyn pressed up against the nightstand appeared in his mind.

That fucking bitc—

Adalyn twirled the heavy ring around her finger as she looked down at it, smiling from ear to ear.

Checkmate, asshole.

YOU'RE JUST AS FUCKED UP AS THE MEN YOU LIKE

With her second class finishing up, Adalyn wondered if Angel even realized she had taken the ring—he had given her no indication all day. She had at least expected a side-eye, but she hadn't even been given that.

She and Lake were the last ones to leave the class. Even their professor had beaten them out for lunch.

"Do you mind if I speak to Adalyn alone?" Angel asked Tom when the girls exited.

Oh God, he knows.

Tom gave him a hard stare before nodding.

"Thanks. We'll catch up with the rest of you in the cafeteria," he reassured him.

When Lake seemed worried, hesitating to walk away, Adalyn tried to give her own reassurance. Truthfully, however, on the inside, she was beginning to shit bricks.

Biting her bottom lip for several minutes as they watched Tom and Lake walk away, she wondered why he hadn't said anything yet. It wasn't until they fully disappeared that she realized why he had waited.

Angel firmly grabbed her by the waist, dragging her backward into the empty classroom.

"Wh-what are you d—"

He spun them in a one-eighty, throwing her back against the door and knocking the breath out of her. Trapping her against the now closed door, Angel pressed his hard body against hers.

"Where is it?" he snapped.

"I don't know what you're—"

He raised a long, tatted finger to her lips. "Lying to me does you no favors."

This was a very dangerous man before her, one who she had to remember was trapped and capable of snapping at any point. *But he is still a dick.*

"Now, tell me where the ring is." He moved his finger to her jaw so she could speak.

She smiled, sweet as pie. "Up your ass."

He moved his hands down her body, going through her coat pockets, then her jean pockets, and then going around to her ass to check the pockets there.

"I'm not stupid enough to carry it on me!" She tried to shoo him away, but he seized her wrists, then plastered them against the door behind her. "Lucca will kill you when I tell him what you're doing to me."

"Probably." Bringing down her wrists, he pulled them roughly behind her back so he could easily hold her in place with one hand. With his now free hand, he lightly gripped the back of her neck, his hot breath caressing her face as he said, "But you won't because you're enjoying our little game too much."

"That's not—"

"Now you're lying to yourself, sweetness." Angel gently grazed her jawline and neck with his lips. "I knew from the second I saw you look at Lucca's that you're just as fucked up as the men you like. You just don't realize it yet."

Adalyn hated herself for knowing he was probably right. That he *was* right. The way he made her body scream out for affection told her that. She was barely grasping her control, wanting to beg him for one kiss.

He now hovered his lips over hers, promising that kiss. "Tell me where the ring is."

Fuck. She desperately wanted to feel his lips on hers, but she couldn't. For once, she finally had Angel right where she wanted him.

"Somewhere you'll never find it."

Clearly losing his patience, he tried again. "That ring doesn't belong to you or me. It belongs to someone very important to me. If you don't give it back, I won't care what I'll have to do to get it."

"I'll give it back to you," she promised, "when you're nicer to me."

The hand around her neck tightened slightly as he pressed his body harder into hers. "Are you sure you wanna do this, sweetness?"

As she smiled up at the mad man before her, every hair on her body stood straight up. It was a sign anyone else would have had when they were frightened, but to her, it was a sign that she was enticed, a sign she had been waiting for.

"Oh, yes."

Angel sat quietly a few tables away, watching the girl who was starting to cause him a lot of trouble eat her lunch. She was turning out to be exactly how he had thought she would when he had witnessed her eyes lighting up at the sight of Lucca.

There was only one fucking problem . . .

He was starting to like exactly that.

She might be really, really, *really* stupid, but she had balls, and he could tell her word meant something to her. It was going to suck when he had to get rid of her, but *she knows too much.*

He wondered if that glint would still be in her eyes if she saw the real Lucca, the boogieman. If that glint would be in her eyes the moment before he slid the knife in her back. It would be a shame if it was; if she appreciated the true darkness and the fucked-up bits of a man.

It was a trait hard to come by, since men like him had only two choices. They either hid that part of themselves, or they were lucky enough to find someone just as fucked up as them.

Ding.

Angel pulled out his phone, looking at the text he had received.

It was a shame about Adalyn, but the fact remained that they both were already taken. The sick part about it was, they both wanted people who didn't want them. Adalyn's heart wanted the boogieman, and he wanted a girl who was in love with his twin brother. A girl he had to hide his true self from.

Still looking down at his phone, he read the message again.

Where are you? I miss you.

HOW DOES IT FEEL TO KNOW YOUR DAYS ARE NUMBERED?

The dead body on the ground stared sightlessly up at the sky as Lucca and Sal stared down at their fallen soldier. Lucca held a cigarette between his lips as he squatted, needing to check the body for any other signs of death. Unfortunately, the bullet in his skull told them all they needed to know.

Dante took a deep breath, sucking in the frigid air and trying to calm the blood that was beginning to boil inside himself. Then he cut the silence between them with his cold tone. "Sal, go see what you can find on the cameras.".

Sal gave a nod before he disappeared.

"Could Angel have done this?" Dante asked once Sal was gone, not wanting to speak about it in front of him.

The fact was: Sal's biological father was Lucifer. And even though Dante had taken him off the streets, Angel was still his brother. A brotherly bond had never formed between him and Lucifer's other children, yet blood was blood.

Lucca took a hard hit off the stick in his mouth, still squatting, carefully examining the body. "I don't know yet."

"Even if it wasn't Angel"—he stared at the body that had been brought to the back alley of his casino hotel, *a message*—"the possibility it was a Luciano is fucking high, especially since we just took out Lucifer."

Standing back up, Lucca started to leave, needing to figure out what had happened.

"I hope she's worth it," Dante told him quietly, unable to hold back any longer.

Lucca stopped instantly as he turned his head back. "What did you just say?"

"That after Drago"—he looked down at the body of one of his best men—"and now Tom, I hope she's worth it."

Turning around, Lucca began to stalk his father, growing closer and closer until he was mere inches away. Then he took the cigarette out of his mouth and blew smoke right into his father's face while putting the butt out right on the chest of Dante's suit jacket. "I'll fucking kill you if you ever speak to me that way again. And we both know I won't hesitate."

The blue-green eyes that stared back at Dante were just as icy and promising as his son's voice. There wasn't a question of whether he would do it. He knew firsthand what Lucca was capable of.

"Understand that, no matter what, Chloe will always be worth it. Even if I have to put a fucking bullet through my own father's brain and bury you six feet under, I will." Dropping the butt to the ground, he dusted off the ashes from his father's jacket, revealing the burnt hole in the expensive Italian suit. "I can take everything from you. Your family, your men, this city. I could take it all tomorrow if I wanted, and no one would question me. They'd follow me because they know what this family could be if I led it."

Dante's jaw flexed as he stared at his creation, what he had brought into this world.

"You're getting old, Father ..." Lucca slightly smiled. "Tell me, how does it feel to know your days are numbered? To know that I could end your reign at any second?"

While he watched his son walk away, he could feel it. The crown he had worn on his head for what felt like most of his life was beginning to slip.

Angel was awoken in the middle of the night by a pair of evil blue-green eyes. He waited for the blade to slit his throat, knowing this had to be the end.

Death had never scared him. It only scared those who had something to lose.

"Get up," Lucca hissed.

What the . . .?

He quickly stood, throwing on some clothes.

"Come, sit down," Lucca commanded, pulling a Zippo out of his pocket.

While Angel took a seat across from Lucca at the small table with two chairs, Sal came in, flipping over objects and going through the room and his shit.

Fuck, she told.

Making sure to keep his cool, his brain began to rack with ways to get out of this.

"You're not gonna ask why we're here?"

Angel stared back, unafraid of the incriminating look Lucca gave him. "I was waiting for you to tell me."

"What did you do today, Angel?"

"I did what I've done every day so far. I wake up, and then Tom and I pick up Adalyn. We go to the school, drop her back off, and then we come back here. I've been in my room since I got back."

When his mattress was flung to the ground and with how thoroughly it was being looked through, he began to understand something had happened.

"What's going on?"

Lucca's eyes didn't waiver from his as he put a cigarette to his lips and flicked open his lighter, not wanting to miss a single expression on Angel's face. "Tom was found in the back alley with a bullet between his eyes."

Fuck.

"And, as far as we know, you were the last one to see him alive."

This was different than stealing a fucking ring. This was the murder of a trusted, respected, and well-loved family member. Hell, even he didn't have a problem with Tom.

Angel was an outsider, someone who didn't belong here, a member of a family whose hatred for the Carusos ran deep. This was some colossal deep shit that had spewed on him, one that could make the Lucianos cease to exist after what Lucifer had done. Their trust hadn't been given yet, and the bridge between them hadn't even been built yet.

Angel squeezed the bridge of his nose, beginning to recollect the events of this afternoon, feeling the weight of his family on his shoulders.

"He dropped me off in the parking garage. When I left him there, he was alive ..." Looking into Lucca's eyes, he let him in, hoping he could see the truth. "I swear to God, he was alive when I left him."

"You sure about that?" Lucca blew smoke into the room.

"Yes. Why the fuck would I kill the man you assigned to watch me?" Angel shut his eyes off to him, having let him see enough. "You're not stupid, Lucca. I know you've figured me out. You know I'm smarter than that. That if I were to kill a Caruso, I wouldn't have picked Tom or dropped him on your doorstep. And we both know I wouldn't have done it with a fucking bullet."

"No, I guess not." Lucca had known guns weren't his style. "But Dominic could have, couldn't he? Went straight through the back of his head and exited out the front. It was one hell of a shot with a pistol." He lifted a finger to point right between Angel's eyes. "One

I've seen only one man pull off from a hundred yards away."

"Dominic didn't do it," Angel assured.

"How do you know if you weren't there?"

Angel smiled. "Because he would have shot him from the front."

Tapping ashes to the ground of the hotel room, Lucca took a long, hard hit, making more of the cigarette turn to ash. "Who do you think did it, then?"

"I should be asking you that question. If anyone would know, it would be you. I've seen you"—he paused, remembering an old memory—"on the opposite side of the tracks, watching us. You've been watching us for years, before you were the underboss, before you became the boogieman."

That comment had Sal pausing from going through Angel's clothes to listen.

"You're good, Lucca. I wouldn't have seen you if you hadn't let me."

He curved one end of his lips; it then disappeared almost before it had appeared. "I don't know what you're talking about."

There was silence in the room for only a moment before Sal's voice broke it.

"He's clean. I can't find anything."

"Be sure to check my phone. I don't want you to miss anything," Angel told them, wanting them to know he had nothing to hide.

Sal gave him a big smile. "I did before I even walked in the room."

"Of course, you did, Salvatore." Angel dragged out his name as he looked at his half-brother, the only son of Lucifer to come out sane. Ironic for the one who had been raised on the streets and taken under Dante's wing. It was poetic, really. The son his father had never wanted had ended up becoming the son he always wanted by the hands of his enemy. Angel wondered if Sal knew who his father was and that he was staring right at his own brother's face.

"I just go by Sal."

"That's not what the rest of the world knows you by," he said before Sal left the room, leaving them alone.

Turning back to Lucca, he couldn't help asking, knowing he of all people had to know the truth, "Does he know?"

Lucca flicked more ashes to the ground. "Why don't you ask him?"

"He's better off not knowing, isn't he?" It wasn't much of a question but a fact between them.

Putting the cigarette out on the table, Lucca warned, "Be careful, Angel. Any little thing you do will be judged from here on out. There will be Carusos who will blame you for this, even if your name gets cleared."

When Lucca began to walk away, Angel almost couldn't believe it.

"So, you believe me?"

Lucca's voice was deadly. "Do you think you'd still be breathing if I thought for a second you did it?"

Not for a second.

When Lucca left, Angel looked around at the disheveled room until his eyes stopped on the nightstand where the ring used to be. If they had found it, it could have been grounds for war. That brat had somehow saved his fucking life.

Well, shit.

MURDER-Y DIFFERENT

Hearing *the news broke her* heart, shattered her. Tom had been watching over her and Lake for a while now, and now he was just … *gone.*

She had heard the whispered accusations toward Angel, but she didn't think he did it. It wouldn't make any sense. At least, she chose not to believe it until she could look him in the eyes again. Then she would know.

If I ever get to see him again.

She doubted they would let him step foot outside the casino hotel anymore.

When the car pulled up to take her to school, her jaw practically dropped to the floor when she saw Angel sitting in the passenger seat. She almost couldn't believe it. It was definitely a good sign he was there, because it meant Lucca didn't think Angel had done it. Lucca didn't take chances with the girls. The ones who watched them were the Carusos' most loyal. That was why she liked Angel although he was a dick to her, because she didn't think Lucca would have picked him to watch her if he didn't have a redeeming quality about him.

Sliding into the car, she took note of the driver. She had met him a couple of times before and remembered his name was Joey.

Seeing Joey as Tom's replacement, it really hit her that he was gone.

"Morning." She tried to keep her voice strong.

Not responding, Joey began to drive with a stone-cold look on his face.

Angel might not have looked at her, but he at least finally said, "Morning, Adalyn."

Looking at him today, he seemed … different. Not murder-y different; just different. Like there was something behind his voice. That maybe he knew she needed to hear a 'good morning' after hearing about Tom.

He probably just wants the ring back.

The rest of the drive was quiet, all of them probably thinking the same thoughts. One thing was for sure, though; she didn't want to know what Joey thought. He seemed different, too, but in his case, it was murder-y different.

Joey parked beside the Escalade that had the rest of the girls waiting for them to arrive. When they got out of the car to meet up with them, they all turned silent when they saw Angel.

"I'm surprised you haven't been killed yet," Maria spoke, not holding back.

Adalyn looked at the faces of the Caruso men, knowing what she meant and why Joey wore such a hateful expression. *They all think he did it.*

"I'm standing here because I didn't do it," Angel told not only her but Joey, the other Carusos, and a somber Lake and Elle.

"That's what my brother says." The tall, leggy blonde looked him up and down. "For now, anyway."

The distaste on the Carusos' faces only grew. You could practically feel the heat of their fury radiating from their bodies, while Angel somehow looked cool and calm.

Maria's heels clicked along the pavement as she walked up to him. "God help you if you had anything to do with it. I'm sure Joey's hands are itching to kill his cousin's murderer."

A low growl came from Joey. "I can't wait."

On Maria's lips was a smile that was almost evil as she and Elle walked away, heading to their classes with their guards. That left the rest of them to walk to their first class.

She's batshit crazy, isn't she?

Starting to walk, she was slightly shocked when she was lightly pulled back by the arm to walk a bit behind Lake and Joey. Angel then pulled her in closer, whispering for only her ears to hear.

"I need to talk to you … alone. Say you want chicken nuggets from the food court and make sure your friends don't follow."

"Okay," she whispered back with a chill from his harshness as he dropped his arm from her and put distance between them once again.

She didn't know what he wanted to speak about, only able to

assume it had to do with Joey. Nevertheless, a part of her had to know. Was she dumb to agree to it? Probably. But nuggets were involved, and that was all she needed.

As they reached the classroom, from Joey's fierce expression, she could only wonder if Angel would still be living and breathing when she came back out. Before heading in, she silently gave him a *good freakin' luck* face.

The second the girls touched their seats, they began talking, with Adalyn leaning over first.

"I need another favor."

"Oh God, not again," Lake groaned, unable to keep any more secrets from Vincent.

"I just need you to not want to get chicken nuggets so I can speak to Angel alone, because I don't think Joey is going to give us many chances," she spoke quickly, as if the favor wasn't a big deal.

"Adalyn, do you think that's safe?"

"He's not going to try anything in a public place. If he does, I'll scream."

Lake nodded, knowing full well she was capable of that. "Do you think he did it?"

Adalyn didn't answer right away, carefully thinking hard about whether he did or not. "I don't think he did."

"Well, that doesn't sound very convincing!" Lake whispered harshly.

"I can't say for certain because I wasn't there, but my gut says no. It really doesn't make sense for him to kill Tom. That's too obvious, if you think about it."

Lake was silent, thinking about her words, clearly knowing what Adalyn said made sense. "I hope for your sake he didn't."

She was confused. "*My* sake?"

"Yes, because you like him; I can tell." Her best friend stopped her before she could object. "And someone as hot as him shouldn't be wasted. Did you ever find out if he can ride a skateboard?"

She began to laugh, figuring it might be more for Lake's sake than hers. "No, but something tells me I shouldn't tell you if I find out he can."

"I think I'd hate you forever if you kept that vision from me."

I actually wouldn't blame you.

"But do me a favor?" Lake asked.

"What?"

"Don't tell me if he can't." Anyone could practically see Angel riding the skateboard in her eyes. "You'll ruin it."

The girls continued to talk about Tom's death during class and throughout the day, trying to figure out who could have done it. One thing was for sure; it didn't look good for Angel or his family.

With their morning classes over, they headed to the cafeteria to meet up with Elle and Maria, finding them both eating salads today.

"Is Maria rubbing off on you, Elle?"

"It's good to have a salad every now and then," Elle told her, but the way she was staring at it, Adalyn wasn't sure if she was trying to convince her or herself.

"Yes, a big, hearty salad with chicken, not a *side* salad," Adalyn corrected her.

"Yeah, I'm gonna get a cheeseburger." Lake gawked at a student who had just sat down with one.

Elle looked over to see what she was staring at. Unable to resist, she said, "Can you grab an extra one for me?"

With them all laughing but one, Maria looked over at her in disappointment. "Weak."

"Don't worry, Elle." Adalyn smiled at her. "I'm weak, too, because I'm going to get chicken nuggets. You all have fun." She quickly turned to leave with Angel, hoping it would be left at that.

"Where do you think you're going, Luciano?" Joey's hard voice was the one who stopped them.

"Taking her to get her nuggets," Angel answered.

He put a hand on Angel's chest, stopping him. "I don't fucking think so."

"Lucca assigned me to her." Looking him dead in the eyes, he kept his voice even. "She's *my* responsibility."

The girls all sat there, stunned at what was unfolding before them. *I like this Angel.*

"I'm not leaving you alone with her."

"Then follow behind us." Angel pushed forward, forcing Joey's hand from his chest.

"I wouldn't even give you the credit card to pay for her food," Joey practically spat at him.

"Don't. I'll pay for it." He shrugged, still walking away.

Practically laughing, Joey couldn't help getting one last dig in. "Your money is dirty."

Angel stopped. Turning around, he came up to Joey, chest to chest, his voice holding a deadly tone now that his family had been brought into it. "Exactly what makes you think your money is clean?"

Adalyn knew what he meant by that. The Carusos didn't earn their money one hundred percent legally either.

"It's cleaner than your family's fuckin' gun money."

"Dirty money is dirty money. And unfortunately for you, you're just as dirty as me."

Joey put his face closer to Angel's. "How do you sleep at night when you hear a kid was killed by a gun your family sold?"

Adalyn's eyes grew wide. She knew the look that was coming upon Angel's eyes. She needed to get him away *now*.

Putting a hand on his arm, she pulled to snap him out of it, thankful when he finally started to walk away.

"Get your fucking hands off him," Joey snapped. "No one's going anywhere. You can either eat a hamburger or a salad like the rest of them, or don't eat at all. I don't really give a shit."

"Like I said, she is my responsibility, so do *not* speak to her that way," Angel threatened as he pushed Adalyn behind him.

"I can speak to her however the fu—"

"Actually, you can't," a soft voice interjected. It wasn't until they all turned their heads to Maria that she continued, "You need to leave *now*."

Oh shit.

Everyone's face, including Angel's, had the same *oh shit* expression that had just filtered through their minds.

There were several awkward moments of silence before Joey managed to nod, then left the cafeteria. You could practically see the steam coming off him from the sheer embarrassment of having *the* Maria Caruso call him out and there was nothing he could do about it.

"Adalyn?"

Swallowing, she looked over at the mafia princess, who unmistakably ruled all. "Yes?"

"Sit down and eat a burger," she said with a snap of her fingers.

One thing Adalyn wasn't ... was stupid. "Okay."

RULES TO LIVE AND DIE BY

Adalyn *and Lake were in* the restroom later that day, drying their hands, when someone who definitely wasn't a woman came through the door.

"What the hell?" Lake sputtered, looking in the mirror at his reflection.

"Angel, *are you crazy?*" Adalyn yelled, looking around to see if anyone else was in there.

"Probably," he told her before looking at Lake. What came out of his mouth next wasn't a request but a demand. "I need you to do something for me."

"What?" Lake answered nervously.

"Watch the door and tell me if that prick starts to come back."

The girls looked confused for a second. Then Lake figured out he meant Maria's bodyguard, who had taken Joey's place.

"You mean Todd?"

"Yeah, him. I think he's trying to fuck some professor, but I need that door guarded."

Okay, maybe Todd is a prick.

Feeling apprehensive, Lake looked at her friend, not knowing if this was a good idea. When Adalyn nodded, though, she gave in, knowing she would be right on the other side of that door if anything happened in there.

Once the door closed with Lake's departure, Adalyn watched Angel move, expecting him to stop in front of her, but he didn't. Instead, he slowly began to walk around her, circling her at a creep-like pace while his eyes danced all over her body. With a chill on her skin, she started to get the feeling she was becoming his prey.

"Wh-what are you doing?"

This time when he went behind her, he lightly scooped some tendrils off her shoulders, bringing them to the front. "Why aren't you afraid of me? Even right now, when you should be, you're not."

Her tongue poked out as she licked her bottom lip while thinking about his words. He was right. Her skin might have gone cold, and nervousness rang in her voice from watching him pace around her, but it wasn't from fear. It was from being awakened. However, she couldn't tell him that.

"You just don't scare me."

"What if I killed Tom?" Those words seemed to echo throughout the room.

Locking her eyes on his when he rounded the front, she went

scarily still. "Did you?"

"I've done a lot of bad shit, sweetness." He opened his shadowed eyes to show her that he wasn't a man of many morals. "But killing Tom wasn't one of them."

The tingle in her skin only heightened. She couldn't explain how or why, but she just knew he was undoubtedly telling the truth. It was like her soul was telling her.

Angel moved in closer, this time stopping right in front of her. Adalyn's breath vanished when he touched her heavy bottom lip with a long finger and began massaging and teasing the sensitive area. Taking one last step forward, he pressed his body against hers as he murmured darkly, "You're lucky you saved my life by stealing the ring."

Her body was screaming now. She couldn't fully comprehend what he was saying. "H-huh?"

A slight smile parted his lips from knowing the effect he had on her. "They searched my room last night and found nothing, because of you, sweetness."

Adalyn didn't know if she should be proud about that fact, but in this moment, in some fucked-up way, she was.

What is he doing to me?

"I guess"—Angel moved his hand down to firmly grab her chin, lifting it high and making her get on her tippy-toes—"I wanted to say thank you."

His warm voice was the last thing she heard before he brought his warm mouth down on hers.

It was a simple kiss, almost innocent, yet it had a roughness to it that shook her to her core. It was like true, utter, sweet bliss; the kind you didn't know existed until you were frightened to death of it ending. It was a feeling she shouldn't be having with a man like Angel and with a kiss like that, which made it the most intimate and beautifully breathtaking thing she had ever experienced.

One that would be impossible to ever forget because it was ...

Simply perfection.

Pulling his lips away from hers, he held her right where he wanted her, keeping a firm hold on her chin, not letting her drop from her toes just yet. There was one last thing he had to say.

"You may have just saved your own life, sweetness, or you may have just cost it." With that, a hazy Adalyn was released.

She watched him walk away, her mind slowly coming back online. She didn't know if he meant taking the ring had saved or cost her her life, or ...

If it had been that kiss.

Shit.

That wasn't what he had planned—to kiss her like that—but she had been so pliable, so submissive underneath him. How she craved a man without morals, one who was evil, corrupt, a man ... like him.

Never before had he met anything like her. Someone who wanted those qualities in a man yet was the complete opposite herself.

Adalyn was pure and fun, but inside, she had a side to her that was desperate to get out. A side that he was capable of bringing out. A side that he had never experienced before because the women he had dealt with were either evil on the outside or too good on the inside.

He could be his true self with her, but it was a commodity that would only come with a high price tag.

There were certain things Luciano men were never supposed to do, a list of rules to live and die by, and kissing her, a Caruso, was on the "do not do" list. One thing was for sure now ...

There will be hell to pay.

FORCE OF A THOUSAND BULLETS

One ... **Two** ... **Three** ... **Four** ... *Angel* didn't know how long it had been since the closet door had been closed.

Five ... Six ... Seven ... Eight ... All he knew was that he was hungry, thirsty, and in pain.

Nine ... Ten ... Eleven ... Twelve ... And even though it was pitch-black in there, he felt like the already tiny space had somehow grown smaller and smaller with each passing hour.

Thirteen ... Fourteen ... Fifteen ... It was almost like a game to see who would crack ...

Crack.

... first. To see who would break ...

Break...

…Before Angel could even awaken enough and move from his bed, one of the masked men was dragging him out of it. The noises he had been hearing was his door being busted in, but his nightmare had been just too strong to be drawn out of it. By this time, it was just too late …

Three men wearing black ski masks were all he could see before he put his arms up to protect his face.

Lying there on the floor of his hotel room, he took the beating of a lifetime.

The obscenities that were thrown around were ones he had heard since birth.

"You fucking piece of shit."

"All you Lucianos are the same."

"Lazy motherfuckers."

"Nasty, tatted bitch."

All words that he had heard repeatedly, words that had been etched on his skin like the tattoos that had been imprinted on his body. Except they went deeper than his tats. They scratched scars into his soul.

There almost wasn't one part of his body that hadn't been hit by the time the masked men stopped to catch their breath. A normal person would have passed out from the pain, but it only made him feel more alive.

"We should have killed every last one of you with your sick fuck of a father."

Angel began to laugh madly through the pain of his injuries as he stared up at the man who had been the most vocal. Remembering that voice, he knew exactly who it belonged to.

"Do you really think you're hiding from me with that mask? Why don't you fucking take it off and face me like a man!" He spat on the ground, blood hitting the man's shoes.

Taking off the mask revealed an intense Joey, who gave him a promise of a lifetime. "I'm going to kill you one day. I'm going to kill every last one of you until the Luciano name doesn't exist."

Any gray in Angel's eyes vanished to the black orbs that now pierced Joey with a force of a thousand bullets that dared him to keep his promise. "We can't fucking wait."

Hearing a noise, Joey slid his mask back on before he and another masked figure headed for the door. The last one, who seemed to be the biggest assailant, stayed back a moment longer to tell the battered Angel one thing.

"I didn't come here for Tom," the devoid voice said as he bent down to take Angel's neck in his hands, his grip slowly beginning to squeeze tighter and firmer "This is for Drago."

With his life fleeing, Angel began to file away every detail he could about the man: his size, his voice, his eyes ...

... Until it all disappeared.

When the Escalade pulled up to her house the next morning, Adalyn's heart sank so deep it almost brought her to her knees. She instinctively knew something was wrong.

It was crazy how something that used to be so normal could now feel so wrong. She thought she missed being picked up in the Escalade with the other girls, but it turned out she didn't at all. Turned out going back to what once was seemed to crumble her future.

"Have you heard anything?" Adalyn's eyes practically begged Lake to know something, anything. Her soul told her that he might be in trouble, which frightened her, and after asking around and going to his hotel room, she came up empty.

It had been three days since she had last seen Angel. Three days since that kiss of a lifetime. And even though she was probably better off without ever seeing him again, she couldn't help wondering what exactly was happening between them. Finding their "little game" enticed her more than anything ever before, she didn't want it to end so soon.

All Lake could do was shake her head solemnly.

"Something bad happened to him." She felt herself breaking down. "I can feel it."

"I think something did," Lake finally admitted as she moved

closer to her friend, keeping her voice down. "Every time I asked Vincent about him, he didn't really answer."

Adalyn swallowed down the vomit that was rising. *Whenever someone goes missing in the mafia, it means only one thing.*

"What if he's—"

"You don't know that yet," Lake tried to console her.

No, Adalyn didn't know that. She didn't know anything; that was the problem. She at least needed to know what happened to him. It was always better to know than not to know.

No matter the cost.

"What are you doing?" Sal asked when Adalyn kept walking.

She didn't open her mouth or turn back, determined to see him.

Sal kept following her. "You can't do that. He's with someone."

"Try me," she barked back at him.

When she raised her hand to pound on the door, Sal tried to stop her, but she kicked him in the nuts.

"What the fuck!"

"Where is he?" She banged on the door as Sal toppled to the ground.

"You little b—"

"I know you're in there, Lucca!" she yelled, continuing to beat the door down.

When the door to his office finally and quickly opened, she

almost hit Lucca's chest.

A very unhappy and furious demon stared her down.

"I'm sorry, but she kicked me in the ... balls." Sal's voice was very high-pitched.

"Where is he?" she asked with a determined expression. She didn't care how scary or how incredibly hot Lucca looked when he was mad; she wasn't leaving until she had answers.

"Leave," was all he said before he began to shut the door, but it stopped when a small body with long, black hair came out from behind him.

A scarred eyebrow rose. "Who?"

Adalyn was shocked that Chloe had appeared from behind him. *Has she been hiding behind him? What are they doing in there? Stay on track, Adalyn!*

"Angel," Adalyn finally answered.

As a slight tinge of hurt appeared in Chloe's eyes at the mention of his name, all Adalyn's furiousness left her. She understood Angel was Lucifer's son, but that wasn't who he was to her.

She felt herself beginning to plead with her. "He's been missing, and no one will tell me where he went."

Chloe stared at her for a moment, then tilted her head up to Lucca. "Where is he?"

Lucca slowly, visibly began to break down. Then he turned his head back to Adalyn, silently killing her with his eyes before he gave in.

"Sal, get up."

Sal managed to stand with his hands protecting his possessions.

"Let her see him," was all he said before the door slammed back in her face.

"Thanks, Chloe!" Adalyn yelled, smiling at the door.

As she turned around to see a very pissed off Sal, it was the first time she had ever seen him mad, which was strange.

Giving him a helpless smile, she tried to laugh. "Sorry. I don't know what got into me."

Silence was all she got.

"Are they … okay?" she asked, recalling how she might have kicked them a little too hard.

"No. No, they aren't." He slightly adjusted himself before walking away.

Oops.

Adalyn followed Sal, not knowing where he was taking her until they got off the elevator on the ninth floor, then went up to a random hotel room. She watched as Sal pulled out a key card from his pocket, then slid it in, unlocking the door.

"Here?" she asked quietly, suddenly nervous, not knowing what to expect on the other side of the door.

Nodding, Sal opened the door for her to go in.

Stepping into the room that looked much like the one Angel had been in before, she practically jumped when the door was closed behind her. Then she tiptoed in farther, not seeing him until the bed came into view. She gasped at the sight, almost unable to believe it.

Walking closer to him, tears beginning to brim her eyes, she saw that he was black and blue all over, severely beaten. Placing a hand on the sleeping Angel's arm, she quickly pulled it back when he jumped awake with a force that didn't look like he should have been capable of in his condition. It seemed as if he had awakened from a nightmare and was ready to fight.

"What the hell are you doing here?" he snapped, slowly trying to sit up and get comfortable. The way he had jarred himself awake hadn't helped his injuries.

"I'm sorry. I didn't mean to scare you. I just ..." Trying to calm her nerves from the fright, she took a breath, wondering if she should admit the truth. Then she did. "I was worried about you."

Staring at her for a moment, he relaxed, losing his harsh expression. "You were worried about me?"

"Yes. I thought something might have happened to you, and it looks like I was right." When she took a step toward him, her eyes got a little cloudy at seeing him like this. There were bruises covering his face and other parts she could see that weren't covered by his T-shirt yet were hard to see from all his dark tattoos.

Noticing her distress, he seemed to take on a different temperament. "I just got beat up a little, is all."

Is he being ... sweet?

She gave a little chuckle as she tried to dry her eyes. "A little?"

He tried to laugh himself but wasn't really capable. "Okay, I might have gotten the shit beat out of me, but to be fair, there were three of them."

"*Three?* Who were they?" She was lucky to be looking at a man and not mashed potatoes.

"It doesn't matt—"

"Yes, it does." She stared at him, realizing it had to be Carusos. "Joey was one of them, wasn't he? What if he does it again?"

That sweet temperament vanished in an instant. "That's my problem, sweetness, not yours. I'll deal with it."

Seeing the look of retribution in his eyes, Adalyn slowly nodded.

"How did you find me? Who even let you in?"

Biting her lip, she debated on telling him the truth. "I may have kicked Sal in the balls trying to talk to Lucca to get him to tell me where you were. Sal let me in." She smiled at the last part.

Amused, Angel curved his lips up, smiling. "Did you really?"

"I did," Adalyn admitted with a laugh. "No one was telling me where you were or where you went, and I couldn't get in touch with you. I thought you might have died."

"Give me your phone," he demanded.

Doing as he asked, she submissively handed it over to him.

Touching the screen, he managed to type with the arm that hadn't gotten hurt too badly. "I'm giving you my number, but know that my phone's being watched, so only contact me if you need me."

"Okay." She felt better now knowing she could find him if he went missing again.

When he handed her phone back, she reached out to grab it, then found herself grabbed and dragged down to the bed to sit beside him. Shocked at first, the second he placed his hand on her jaw, she melted into it.

"Adalyn, there's something else I need from you." His tone

turned as dark as his eyes that now bore into her. "I put an address in your phone under my contact."

Her heart was pumping out of her chest not sure if she was liking where this was going.

"If anything happens to me, I need you to make sure that my friend and my friend only gets the ring."

Shaking her head, she didn't like what he was saying. "Nothing's going to happen to you."

He slowly grazed his knuckles against her cheek. "I don't belong here, sweetness; you know that."

He had told her so simply, and she knew he was right, as sad as that fact was. She remembered what she had told him herself when she first met him. *You're in enemy territory.* For as long as he was there, he would never be safe.

Nodding, she agreed to do it for him.

"Promise me." He didn't ask but ordered to hear it from her.

Whispering her promise, she gave him what he wanted. "I promise, Angel."

"Thank you." He smiled and continued his motion only for a second longer before he let her go. "You better go before Sal or Lucca come back to check on you."

"Am I going to see you again?" Adalyn bit her lip, not wanting to leave his side. She didn't know what this meant for Angel, if or when he could go back to watching her at school, or even if Lucca would allow it, considering the Carusos hated him so badly.

"I don't know when I can see you again, but I'll find you,

sweetness," he made his own promise this time. "I still need the ring you stole from me, remember?"

"Oh, yeah." She smiled, *but you're definitely not getting it back anytime soon.*

Taking a breath, assured she would see him again, she started to leave, but then she remembered she at least needed a name for who to return the ring to.

"What's your friend's name?"

Getting up from his bed, hurt and stung by the name he had given her, she walked away from him.

Hearing that name had burned her soul. It was in the way he had said it, the way he had formed that beautiful name, the way it had sounded as it had passed his lips, and the look in his eyes as it did. It was something only a woman would understand when the man she was falling for said another woman's name.

It was a name she wouldn't ever forget, no matter how desperately she wanted to.

Bella.

I AM AND WILL ALWAYS BLEED LUCIANO BLOOD

"How do you feel?" *Lucca* asked, taking a seat in the corner of the room.

Angel didn't even turn his head to look at him, knowing who it was. "How the fuck do you think? Your men almost beat me to death."

Flicking his lighter on and off, he started to twirl the fire between his fingers. "Sorry about that."

Damn fucker wasn't even apologizing for his men.

"Can you name them?" he asked, flicking his lighter closed.

Angel looked at him then, knowing exactly why he wanted to know. *And let you have all the fun?* "No."

Nodding, Lucca stood, going over to him so he didn't have to use energy to look at him. "I promise you this, it won't happen again."

"So, I guess you're still not letting me go." He sunk back in the bed, defeated. He at least thought getting the shit beat out of him was going to give him a get-out-of-jail-free card.

"I can't do that. Not until our families find peace again, and not until I find out who killed Tom."

Fuck. He was going to be surrounded by Carusos forever.

"I can, however, start treating you like one of my men," Lucca said simply.

Shocked, Angel didn't know if he had heard him correctly. "What?"

"Starting tomorrow, you will be a soldier for the Caruso family and will be compensated as such for the time being. This means you answer to me or my father." The last part was the most important that came with a warning from the underboss. If he was to agree, it would mean he would now bleed and die for the Carusos, who he was now working for, who he had been led to believe were his sworn enemies his entire existence. Then again, beaten, bloodied, and trapped didn't give him much of a choice. His blood was Luciano, and there was no changing that.

Angel nodded, silently hoping that consenting wouldn't come back to haunt him.

Before Lucca could leave, there was something he wanted. "I have a condition."

"What is it?"

Staring Lucca down, he let him know it would be a deal breaker. "I do my job and protect Adalyn *without* one of your men watching me."

"Fine." Lucca glared back, his voice taking a deadly turn. "You betray my trust, though, Angel, it will be the last thing you ever do."

ONE WEEK LATER

As she walked outside, the air seemed crisper. It was going to start snowing anytime now. Adalyn would welcome some change right now. It had been one long week since she had seen Angel last; she just hoped he was still breathing.

School didn't seem the same anymore without him. Truth be told, her life didn't seem the same anymore without him. He had ended up being the surprise of her lifetime, and she truly felt he had changed her life forever. There were some people who could do that to you, even if you had only met them for a second. You just could never forget them.

Waiting for the Escalade to pull up, she was shocked to find that it never did. Instead, it was the car Tom had used to pick her up.

Great, another one.

It wasn't until the car pulled up right next to her that she was able to see who it was through the dark tint.

Angel, wearing sunglasses, rolled down the passenger window when she just stood there in shock. "Are you going to get in, sweetness?"

"You're still alive," she whispered, still stunned, never in the slightest having expected him to come back so soon.

When she still didn't get in, he opened his door and got out to go to the other side. Amused, he opened the passenger door for her. "I'm a lot harder to kill than that."

Her lips turned up in a smile, and she was finally able to get in the car. "I can see that."

Watching him close her door before getting back in, she could see by his slow movements that he still wasn't back to normal, and looking at his profile now, she could see why he was wearing the big shades—his face was still bruised.

Still staring at the bruises, she actually hurt for him. "Does it hurt?"

"No," he answered truthfully. "Pain isn't really an issue for me."

Looking at his inky hands as he turned the steering wheel, she knew he had to be a freak. "I bet not with that many tattoos."

"I enjoy getting tatted," he admitted with a half-sinister smile.

I knew it.

"How many do you have?"

"Too many to count."

Her brow rose as she became too curious for her own good. "How covered are you?"

He was silent a moment before he answered, "Almost completely."

That didn't help her imagination. It only made her want to know how much of a freak he was. However, she figured it wouldn't be polite to ask if his ass or dick was tatted, too, so she asked a reasonable question instead. "How old were you when you got your first one?"

"Sixteen."

"*Sixteen?* Is that even legal?" No wonder he was already covered in tattoos.

Smiling, he laughed. "With a parent's permission, yes. But in my case, it was illegal. I have a great tattoo artist, though, so it came out good."

"Did you get in trouble?"

"No. Tattoos aren't a big deal in our family. Almost everyone has them."

"Oh." The Lucianos were a lot different than the Carusos; that was for sure.

With silence filling the car and now that her shock at seeing him had worn off, she realized that he alone was taking her to school.

"No one else came with you?"

He looked in the rearview mirror at the cars following behind him. "Lucca's agreed to trust me, but I assume I'm still being watched."

Lucca's agreed to trust him? "So, what does that mean?"

"He asked me to work for him legitimately while I'm here." *Well,* here *as in* forced *to be here.*

"Really?" She almost couldn't believe it. It was unheard of.

Angel nodded as he pulled into the parking spot beside the Escalade.

"So, it's like you're kinda a Caruso?"

Looking at the girls' and the Carusos' faces that were a mixture of disbelief and disgust said it all. "No, I am and always will bleed Luciano blood."

SHIT THAT ONLY HAPPENS
IN ROMANCE NOVELS

L ake and Adalyn looked at each other when Angel didn't stay outside the door but instead followed them into their classroom.

"What are you doing?" Adalyn asked when he ended up taking a seat behind them.

Angel reclined back in his seat, getting comfortable. "I don't want to stand outside like a dog. I can watch you both better from here, can't I?"

"He's right," Lake said, agreeing too easily with him.

Narrowing her eyes, she stared at her friend. *You just want to look at him.* "I'm not sure if he's allowed."

The end of his lip tilted up. "It's a big class in a big college, sweetness; no one's gonna notice an extra person."

Lake practically swooned when she heard him say *sweetness*. "Yeah, no one will notice."

Adalyn had to contain herself from rolling her eyes at her friend and at Angel, who seemed to be getting a kick out of Lake agreeing with him.

Looking toward the front, she could see the girls glancing back to get a look at him as well. He was hard not to fucking miss, considering he stood out like a sore thumb with all his tats. Her friend was one of those girls, too, who couldn't look away and hadn't turned her head back toward the front to mind her own fucking business.

"Are you not in pain?" Lake asked, concerned about his bruises and his condition.

Angel made a slight wince behind his shades. "A litt—"

"He's fine," Adalyn sharply cut off his charades while glaring at them both.

"Adalyn, quit being so rude! Look at him. He's clearly in pain." Lake tried to get closer to see the bruises on his face when he raised his sunglasses.

"Oh, he'll be hurting when I get Lucca to take a baseball bat to his ass," she muttered angrily to herself under her breath.

"Did you say something?" Lake asked her when Angel had abruptly placed the shades back on his face.

Giving a fake-ass smile, she silently murdered them both in her head. "Yeah, I said *poor baby*."

"Who would do that to you?" Lake asked in a nurturing voice.

I wish I did.

"I don't know, Lake. Maybe you should ask your *boyfriend*," Adalyn emphasized with another fake-ass, million-dollar smile to, you know, remind her that she had a *fucking boyfriend*!

Lake snapped her head back to the front then, before quietly speaking after clearing her throat. "I'll do that."

Adalyn, on the other hand, looked back at a content Angel, whose eyes were clearly grinning behind his shades. *That's it. I hate him again. And you . . .* She turned her head back to her friend and opened her mouth for only her to hear. "So you know . . ."

Lake was practically in daydream land, fantasizing about Angel being on a skateboard again, but she managed to look over at Adalyn to hear what she had to say.

Sitting up straight, her face took on a very smug turn, proud for the words that were about to come out of her mouth. "He can't."

Slumping over, it was like all the air had been let out of her as Lake rested her chin on her hand. "Thanks a lot."

"No problem." Adalyn continued to sit there, feeling smug, not caring if she had told a lie or not. Truthfully, she hadn't asked him yet. Either way, she wasn't going to let Lake find out if he could.

Now aggravated, she felt like the class seemed to creep by and, with Angel sitting behind her, she couldn't sit comfortably, feeling him staring at her back. She couldn't wait for it to be over, and when it finally was, she stood up suddenly, grabbing her things and quickly leaving that cramped room.

They had to catch up to her; Lake had to practically jog.

"Will you slow down?" Lake huffed once she reached her.

"I was giving you alone time with boyfriend number two." Adalyn didn't bother lowering her voice.

Lake did care if he heard as he was following just a short distance behind them, whispering over to her, "I'm sorry. I can't help it. It's the sunglasses. He looks like someone I met while I was in Treepoint, Kentucky—"

"Oh God, not this story again." Rolling her eyes, she did not want to hear this fictional bologna again. Grabbing her by the shoulders, she gave Lake a little shake. "We've told you before; super sexy, hot guys in motorcycle clubs is shit that only happens in romance novels, especially when they're covered in tats and have names like Razer and Viper."

"It really happen—"

"Were any of them ugly or even a little bit overweight?" Adalyn asked in all seriousness.

Lake had to think about it a second. "No ..."

"See? Fictional!" She let her go and kept walking. "Your crazy-ass grandparents probably just slipped you some of their crazy pills, is all."

Lake wasn't going to let it go. Looking behind her, she made sure to keep her voice down. "Angel's covered in tats, and he's hot."

"Yeah, but this is real life, and he doesn't drive a motorcycle."

"Ooo ... maybe he does. We should ask him."

Adalyn grabbed her friend's arm, squeezing it like the jaws of life.

"Or not!" Lake said in a high-pitched squeal, pulling her arm back. "I'm just trying to prove my point that it really happened to me. I wonder if his brothers and the rest of the Lucianos are attractive. Then maybe you might believe me."

Hmm … That might be something she could get behind, considering Angel wasn't working out for her anymore. Quickly glancing back at him, she honestly couldn't be mad at her friend. Angel was like a rare gem in their world with his tattoos.

"No way. I bet he got all the looks in his family. It would be another romance novel if any one of them looked anything like him."

"Yeah, you're probably right," Lake said in defeat. "I'm sorry if I upset you. You know I love Vincent. I'm just excited for you 'cause he's the first one you've liked who doesn't have a girlfriend. Plus, we talk about Lucca all the time, so I didn't think you would care. I won't talk about how good-looking he is again," she promised.

"First off, I don't like him anymore." She paused when Lake was the one to roll her eyes. "And secondly, you're right. I know you don't mean anything by it because, if you had picked someone hot who wasn't my brother, I would probably act the same way, too." And that was the truth. She just didn't like how Angel was milking the fact that Lake obviously found him attractive.

"You mean, you would be acting like me but times a thousand."

Okay, that may be true, too.

She laughed; there was no denying it. "Probably."

Happy that they were friends again, Lake got serious, wanting to be on her friend's good side. "Okay, so we hate Angel again, got it?"

Adalyn nodded triumphantly. "Yes, we do."

Walking into their next class and taking their seats, Angel lazily sat behind them again.

Before class could start, a huge pair of boobs entered her view and a girl who could almost rival Maria as a supermodel stopped in front of her.

"Is he your boyfriend?" she asked Adalyn while staring at Angel like she wanted to rip his clothes off. She had also asked the question loud enough to where he could easily hear.

Looking at her strangely, Adalyn couldn't believe this girl had asked her that. "Um ... no."

"Good." She beamed, already going up to him. "Would you like to go out som—"

"No thanks," Angel cut her off in a cold voice without even looking at her.

Blinking with holy-fuck-did-that-even-happen, that-shit-was-cold, I'm-a-heterosexual-girl-and-even-I-looked-twice faces, both Lake and Adalyn couldn't believe what they were witnessing when the girl walked away, practically in shame. Turning their heads to look at each other, they could only stare at the other in shock for a few minutes.

Okay, maybe we are *in a romance novel.*

Swallowing hard, Lake looked like she was getting hot as she tried her best to whisper over, "So, we like him again?"

"Definitely."

I COULD SHOW YOU
SOMETIME, SWEETNESS

All the girls decided to eat in the cafeteria, considering it was a pizza day. Even Maria had thrown her salad out the window to eat a slice.

"What happened to him?" Elle asked, eyeing Angel at where he sat a few tables away. She was clearly out of the loop.

"He got beat up," Adalyn told her simply, not sure if she could give more information than that. They were all Carusos, and the mafia princess was sitting at the table.

Putting down her pizza, the girl who didn't want to be around him due to her friend being captured by the Lucianos, Elle almost seemed concerned. "Who did that to him?"

Does he just get irresistible when he's hurt or something?

Not knowing what to say to her, Adalyn tried to skate around it. "Uh ... I'm not—"

"Carusos," Maria told her, throwing down her pizza. It was almost unexpected the way she had said it. For a girl who really didn't like him and who had strong roots to the family she loved so much, there was a bit of disdain in her voice when she had said the family name.

Elle seemed appalled. "Really? Which ones?"

Looking over at Maria, Adalyn wondered if she knew. When she didn't answer, though, Adalyn simply shrugged, not wanting to speak Joey's name. "Don't know yet."

"I wonder if Nero would know?" Elle's eyes hadn't moved from him.

"I'm going to ask Vincent, too," Lake agreed, also staring at him.

For Christ's sake, what is happening? They already have sexy, hot men! Especially Elle! Nero is Lucca's only slightly less hot brother! That family had something weird in their blood, like they descended from God Himself. She looked over at Angel now. *And he was created by Satan! Okay ... maybe by a really, really good-looking Satan, but still! Shit, he is hot.*

It took everything Lake had to look away from him. "Maria, I have a question."

"Yes?" the blonde who was also descended from God answered.

"Have you seen any of Angel's brothers or the other Lucianos?"

"A few. Why?"

Not wasting time, Lake got right to the point. "Are they hot?"

Adalyn found herself scooting to the edge of her seat, waiting for the next words out of Maria's mouth. Even Elle leaned in closer, her interest piqued, too.

Flipping her hair behind her shoulder, Maria then picked up her pizza. "Nope."

"Told ya." Adalyn smiled righteously over at a soul-crushed Lake before taking a big bite out of her pizza.

That shit's for fairy tales.

Leaving the last class of the day, Adalyn didn't know how she felt about Angel anymore. She liked him, and then she didn't, especially when he ignored her like he used to when they were in the cafeteria. He had only paid attention to her when Lake was around.

Jerk.

On the way to the car, her eyes were drawn to the guy who had tried to run into her on the skateboard, along with some guys behind him, who had been laughing and watching that day. They were giving her and Lake uncomfortable feelings with their glances.

"You girls all alone today?" The skateboarder stepped closer.

Angel came up behind them, walking in the middle as he placed his arm around Adalyn, showing him that they weren't.

The skater looked shocked for a moment to see him again, not recognizing him at first. Then he noticed his rough appearance. He continued following them from a short distance away with his group backing him up.

"I was wondering what happened to you. Should have known someone put you in your place."

Continuing to pull the girls along, Angel acted like they didn't exist.

When they didn't stop following them, Adalyn started to get pissed. "Will you fuck off—"

Pulling her into his side, Angel shut her up.

Walking in front of them, the skateboarder stopped dead in his tracks, forcing them to stop abruptly, too. "What did your bitch just say?" There was a look in his eyes that told her she had pissed him off.

Excuse me? His bitch?

"I believe she said to fuck off," Angel answered in a threatening tone.

With the skater's friends circling them, he stepped up to Angel. "That wasn't smart. You look worthless right now."

"I would think really fucking hard if you want to do this, kid, because I got nothing to lose. I don't go to school here, and I wouldn't give a shit if I couldn't step foot back on campus."

Some of his friends backed up, knowing he was right. There was an audience of students watching them now. They wouldn't be able to lie about not starting the fight.

The skater looked around, seeing all the eyes on him, and with his backup not willing, he was at a loss. "I want my board back." He smirked before his eyes moved to Adalyn, who Angel still had his arm around. "Because to me, it looks like you do have something to lose."

Angel dropped his arm from Adalyn's shoulders, then went up

to him, showing the kid he was no longer playing games and that, even injured, he was well enough to take him on right now. "You should have thought about that before you tried to run her over with it, fucker."

You could see the skater contemplate hitting him for a second, right before he chickened out and walked away. "Next time, then."

"Pray there won't be," Angel advised with a lethal promise.

Disgusted at what had taken place, Adalyn waited until the prick left before she gave her opinion. "What an asshole."

"What the hell's wrong with him?" Lake agreed.

"Don't ever speak to him again," Angel ordered Adalyn before looking at Lake. "Either one of you."

Lake agreed easily, nodding her head, but Adalyn didn't. She didn't like how he had shut her up from telling the asshole to fuck off.

Not about to take his order, she walked off, heading back to the car like she had been trying to before the dickhead had stopped them. *I can tell him to fuck off if I want.*

After all of them were quiet for the rest of the walk, Lake got in the already filled Escalade, while Adalyn went straight to the car door. However, Angel wouldn't unlock it, waiting until the Escalade pulled off before he finally hit the remote's button that unlocked the car doors.

As soon as she heard the locks disengage, she threw open the car door, about to get in, when a hand came around her belly, firmly holding her in place. She froze when he spanned his fingers across her taut skin and pressed his lean body into her back.

Leaning down, he whispered softly into her ear, "Why did you walk away from me, sweetness?"

"B-because I'm not agreeing to that." God, she really hoped she could stay strong, but she seemed to always mold to him when he was like this.

Angel flipped her around in a swift motion, smiling down at her shocked yet thrilled expression. There seemed to be a glint in his eyes as he taunted, "Your friend agreed with me easily enough."

Her hasty reply came with a grin. "That's because she finds you attractive."

"Are you saying you don't find me attractive?" He moved a finger up her neck to the tip of her chin, forcing her to face him when she answered.

Swallowing, she lied, "No."

"What have I said about lying, sweetness?" He leered down at her, knowing her too well.

"I didn't," she helplessly lied again. "You seemed to like her this morning. Maybe you should leave me alone and bug her instead."

"I can't do that because I don't like her." He moved his lips to the skin above her jaw. "I like you."

Don't be weak, Adalyn!

"Well, I don't like you."

Moving closer to her lips, he was so close to kissing her again. "You sure?"

"Mmhmm."

"Okay, then." He pulled his face from hers, standing straight up and far from her reach.

Her body practically cried out in pain. "W-wait …"

"Yes?"

"I might like you a little," she confessed softly.

His tone becoming more serious, he wasn't going to give in. "Then if you like me, you'll promise not to mouth off to him ever again."

"But he deserves it—"

"He deserves a hell of a lot more than that," Angel told her fiercely, not moving his eyes from hers. "But I know people like him, Adalyn. They feed off your anger. They want a reason to hurt you. Telling them off gives them that. You saw how he reacted when you said something. I've learned ignoring them doesn't give them that chance."

Remembering how Angel had reacted, not saying anything until she had told him to fuck off, she realized he might be right. Her mind wasn't happy about it, but her body really freaking wanted that kiss.

"Fine, I promise."

Giving a slight smile, he slowly lowered his head toward hers. Taking her bottom lip between his teeth, he gave a delicate pull before releasing it.

Adalyn could have died in that moment, loving the way it felt to be captured by him. Anticipating what else was to come, she squeezed her thighs together as a wave of heat flowed through her lower belly.

"Good." He lightly tapped her ass with the hand that had been resting at the small of her back. "Now, get in."

Her jaw almost dropped to the floor and the breath she had

been holding released in a huff as he pulled away from her reach. She should have guessed he would do that.

Deciding to file that away for later, she got in the car, somewhat grateful he hadn't really kissed her. *Because God knows if I would've stopped.*

She watched him get in and start the car; it was strange seeing an almost playful attitude come from him today. She was unable to stop smiling almost the entire way to her house. She had to admit their "little game" sure was fun.

"What did you mean this morning when you said *he can't* to Lake?"

She had to practically shake her head before realizing what he was talking about. "Oh, we wanted to know if you knew how to ride a skateboard, but I told her you couldn't."

"I do know how to ride, though." He laughed as he put the car in park once he reached her driveway.

Well … shit. Her cheeks began to turn a bright shade of pink as she reached for the car door and opened it. With visions of him skateboarding, she damn sure didn't trust herself to be around him.

A slow smile appeared on his lips. "I could show you sometime, sweetness."

LEAVE, ADALYN!

Getting out of the car quickly, she stopped before turning back to make one last mistake. "You don't ride a motorcycle, though, right?"

"No, but I know how. I used to ride dirt bikes a lot, but I haven't ridden in a whil—"

Slamming the door, she looked heavenward. "Why, God, why?"

THE MOMENT RIGHT BEFORE HE BROKE

Through the huge glass window, she stared down at the city below her while tapping her heels. She had waited for what seemed like an hour before the door behind her finally opened.

Without turning around to see who it was, she spoke to the air, almost like she was speaking to the universe. "What is it that makes a person just"—lifting manicured fingers, she snapped them—"*snap?*"

"Who are we talking about?" Lucca asked, stopping beside her to stare out at the city.

Truthfully, she wanted to know why anyone would, but right now, she would settle on just one. "Joey."

Not wanting to beat around the bush, he got on with it. "What did you come here for, Maria?"

"I want to know what you're going to do with him."

"I haven't decided yet."

"And the others? Do you know who they were?" A hard expression seeped onto the pretty blonde's face.

"What does it matter to you?" Lucca looked at his sister. "I thought you didn't like Angel."

Her heartless voice matched her heartless soul. "I don't, but I don't like traitors either."

"Neither do I," he agreed, looking back out at the city.

"So, who were they?"

With a sigh, he didn't seem pleased when he responded, "I haven't figured that out yet either."

Shaking her head, she looked at him from the corner of her eyes. "I think you might be losing your touch, brother."

"And you think you could do better?" Amused by his own question, he didn't anticipate his little sister's reply.

"Oh, I know I could," she told him without an inkling of a doubt in her mind. She turned around to face him, not letting him underestimate her. "Do you really think you would be the one to sit on the throne if I weren't born a woman?"

Lucca's intense blue-green eyes had a question of his own. "Do you know what rules are for, Maria?"

Now it was his reply that she hadn't anticipated.

"They are meant to keep weak men from breaking, and given for great men to break."

One ... Two ... Three ... Four ... Angel didn't know how long it had been since the closet door had been closed.

Five ... Six ... Seven ... Eight ... All he knew was that he was hungry, thirsty, and in pain.

Nine ... Ten ... Eleven ... Twelve ... And even though it was pitch-black in there, he felt like the already tiny space had somehow grown smaller and smaller with each passing hour.

Thirteen ... Fourteen ... Fifteen ... It was almost like a game to see who would crack first. To see who would break first. Either his father would by unlocking the door, or Angel's mind would break before his father even came to the door.

The best part of the game was that neither of them would know who won until the door opened. It was a sick game of outlast, and they both would be damned if they lost.

Sixteen ... Seventeen ... Eighteen ... The counting helped to keep him sane. He didn't know how many times he had started back at one, but it kept his mind occupied when he couldn't sleep in the darkness.

A crack of light finally showed under the door, giving him a little glimmer of brightness. Thinking his father had come into the room, he thought he was finally free.

It wasn't until a piece of candy was slid under the door that he realized he was far from saved.

Angel just stared at the candy with a tear streaming down his face.

"Are you holding up in there, Angel?" Dominic's worried voice came through from the other side when he didn't take it.

Wiping away the tear, he took the gift. "I'm okay," he managed to get out of his dry throat.

"Suck on it for as long as you can; it'll help."

He unwrapped the hard piece of red, glossy candy; the cherry flavor exploded in his mouth and his dry throat started to produce saliva.

The shadow under the door showed his brother was still there.

"How's Matthias?"

Silence grew until Dominic finally answered, "He's better."

That answer gave him a shiver up his spine. Not until he was set free would he know if his twin came out all right on the other side.

"You're different than him." Dominic's voice was almost ominous, like it didn't belong to a teenage boy. Then again, a boy like him had never gotten to be a kid, let alone a teenager. There were five years between them. Five long years Dominic had had to spend on this earth alone with the devil. How he had survived, no one knew. No one even knew if Dominic had the answer to that. "You have to be the strong one, Angel. You might not break if he does. But if you break, he breaks."

His words of wisdom were all he left him with when he walked away, leaving him to the darkness.

It wasn't until hours later, with those words swirling through his head, that he realized the severity of them.

To keep his twin meant to protect Matthias and sacrifice himself to the darkness. It was something he had done once, but now he understood he was going to have to do it every time. Matthias's weakness would have to become his strength. His fear would have to become Angel's friend.

Placing his little hands on the door, he felt around, tracing the walls around him. With each touch, what were once walls had slowly become his cage.

As he breathed heavily, the trapped feeling started to close in around him. If he was lucky, he would be in there until the moment right before he broke. The next time, he could only hope he could last longer, and longer, repeatedly, each time being released right before he lost it all. Then maybe one day . . .

. . . A sweaty Angel awoke from another nightmare. Knowing he'd had too many in a row, he made himself get up off the bed and grabbed his pillow.

Staring at a sliding door, he finally slid it open to reveal a closet.

Angel threw his pillow down on the closet floor before going in and lying down on the floor.

The hard surface hurt his injuries at first, but then he managed to get somewhat comfortable enough to sleep. It wasn't until he slid the door closed again and caged himself in that he greeted his old friend.

It was funny a thing . . . When he pulled his hands from his cage, the darkness didn't allow him to see it. It was only there if he decided to reach out and touch it.

YOU FUCKERS ARE UGLY

O pening the door, Adalyn walked into the beautiful, dark apartment.

"Do you know how to knock?" Vincent grumbled from the sofa.

"Yes, I just don't want to." Heading over to the sofa, she decided to be an even more pain in the ass by trying to squish herself between him and Lake.

"There's a whole damn couch, Adalyn!" He tried to fight off his sister, but with Lake laughing instead of trying to help, he gave up and got up off the couch. "You're fucking driving me crazy!"

Satisfied, she sunk into the couch, lying down and placing her head on Lake's lap. "I'm just trying to hang out with *my* best friend."

"Well, she's *my* girlfriend!"

"That's irrelevant. She was my BFF first."

"Lake, aren't you going to say anything?" Vincent looked at her for help.

"I mean …" Lake's eyes went back and forth between them, not knowing what to say at first. "We were best friends for years before I started dating you."

Adalyn snickered. "Yeah, 'cause you were too busy whorin—"

"I'm going upstairs before I kill you."

"Bye!" she yelled up at him as he walked up the stairs.

Lake lightly hit Adalyn's shoulder. "That wasn't very nice."

"I wasn't wrong, was I?"

"Well …" Lake narrowed her eyes, thinking about all the girls who had thrown themselves at Vincent over the years.

"The truth hurts," Adalyn answered for her.

Laughing, Lake started to run her fingers through Adalyn's hair as she lay on her lap, waiting until Vincent was out of earshot. "So, how was the car ride home with Angel yesterday?"

Her face blushed a shade of pink again, remembering what he had said. "Fine."

"Tell me!" Noticing the color of her cheeks, Lake knew something had happened.

"Nope. No more Angel fantasies for you."

"Come on, Adalyn. I would tell you. At least give me something!"

You can't tell her that he can ride a skateboard 'cause then you'd be a liar, and you definitely can't tell her he can ride a motorcycle because I'm pretty sure she'd leave Vincent for him.

Settling on something, she gave her friend a wink. "He's a

great biter."

"Oh God. You lucky bi—"

"What are y'all talking about?" Vincent asked, coming back down the stairs.

"I was just asking Lake if she wanted to go see the new *Jumanji* movie tonight."

"Oh yes, I've been dying to see it." Lake practically forgot they had been discussing Angel. "Will you take us, Vincent?"

"Hell no. I gotta work," he told her, throwing on his jacket before walking to Lake to give her a kiss goodbye.

"Ew." Adalyn had a full view of them pecking each other on the lips from where she lay.

"Why don't you go ask Elle and Nero if they wanna go? Nero can watch you all." He practically cackled all the way out the door at the thought of getting back at his best friend.

Adalyn practically jumped up from the couch. "Sounds good to me. Let's go."

Grabbing her jacket and their things, the girls went out the door a few minutes behind Vincent. All they had to do was knock on the next door and, in just another minute, Nero answered.

Adalyn's eyes practically lit up at seeing the gorgeous green-eyed Caruso brother.

"We were wondering if you and Elle wanted to go see *Jumanji*?"

Nero started to close the door. "No than—"

"Oooo ... I do! Can we please go?" Elle ran to the door, begging him.

Running a hand through his hair, he seemed to quickly think on his feet. "Actually, I can't. I have to work."

"Maybe Amo will take us?" Adalyn asked.

Both Nero and Elle answered in unison, "He won't."

Okay . . .

Not wanting to be the last resort, Nero quickly grabbed his jacket, gave Elle a kiss, and headed to work, just like Vincent had.

"You two need new boyfriends," Adalyn huffed, out of ideas. "What are we going to do now?"

"Let's ask Chloe to go. Lucca might take us." Elle closed the door behind her, crossing the hall to knock on the other door. When no one answered, she pulled out her phone and put it to her ear. She was only on the phone for a few seconds before she hung up, seeming a little confused. "They're at Lucca's house. She said they're gardening?"

"It's practically winter," Adalyn stated the obvious, knowing it had been a lie. *A fucking horrible one.* "Let's just steal Nero's keys and take ourselves."

"You know we can't do that anymore, Adalyn. It's not safe," Elle remind her.

Knowing she was right, especially with the Lucianos and Tom's death, she still didn't like it.

"This is bullsh—"

"I know! We can ask Maria; she comes with bodyguards," Lake interrupted proudly.

Elle put her phone to her ear again and, not even a second later, a door all the way down on the other end of the hall opened, Maria motioning them to come to her.

The girls all walked down and entered the apartment the Caruso family stayed in from time to time.

"I have to call Lucca and ask if we can go with just my two men," Maria told them before he picked up her phone. She, too, was only on the phone for just a few seconds. "He said we needed one more man if we're all going to go, but since it's Saturday and he didn't plan for us to go out, they're all busy."

"Great," Adalyn muttered, their plans all ruined because the boys would rather work than take them to a movie. "If I had a boyfriend and he didn't take me, I would break up with him."

"I'm not breaking up with Vincent," Lake told her for what seemed like the thousandth time.

"Yeah, they had to go to work," Elle added.

Rolling her eyes so hard they practically popped out of there socket, Adalyn snarked, "Sure, they did."

"I have an idea." Maria called Lucca again, making them listen to her plan by asking him, "What if Angel wanted to go?"

Adalyn's jaw almost hit the ground. The mafia princess wanted a Luciano to take them?

"Are you serious?"

Lake's eyes lit up. "Good idea."

Of course, you'd think so.

"Yeah." Elle's eyes lit up as well.

No, not you, too! I'll never have a chance with him!

When she hung up the phone, Maria smiled at Adalyn. "Lucca

said, if we ask him and he wants to, then we can go."

She was starting to get uncomfortable. "Why are you staring at me like that?"

"'Cause you're going to ask him."

"*Why me?*"

"He's *your* boyfriend, not mine," Maria told her, holding the door open. "Lead the way."

"He's not my boyfriend," she corrected as she headed out the door. *I might wish, though.*

All the girls and Maria's two bodyguards headed toward Angel's room now.

When they got off the elevator, she suddenly and strangely got a little nervous as she reached his door.

"Guys, it's Saturday. He's probably busy and doesn't want to deal with us. He had to all week."

The tall blonde forced her along. "Do you want to see the movie or not?"

Biting her lip, Adalyn stared at the door while they waited a few feet away. Unsure whether to do it or not, she eventually said, *fuck it*, and knocked on the door.

Only a few moments passed before the door was suddenly opened and a sinisterly smiling Angel appeared.

It was hard for her to concentrate on what she had come here for, considering he was just wearing jeans and a dark-colored T-shirt that exposed many of his tattoos.

Lake and Elle were practically breaking their necks for a better glimpse of him.

When she continued to stare, Angel tried to help her out. "Yes?"

"Sorry, um." She cleared her throat, trying to get her thoughts under control. "We wanted to go to the movies, but we kinda need one more person to watch all of us in order to go. No one else wants to, so basically, I was wondering if you wanted to see a movie with us?"

"Sure. Give me a second," Angel answered instantaneously.

Having expected rejection, her jaw hit the ground for the second time today when he went back inside to grab his things.

"Wait … Is he your boyfriend?" Elle began to wonder.

"No," she whispered back, evil eyeing Maria for saying that earlier.

"Maybe we do need new boyfriends, then," the strawberry-blonde admitted, starting to get a little mad that Angel had easily agreed, while Nero would rather work than take them.

Angel opened the door and came back out, wearing a plain, dark gray sweatshirt. "So, what are we going to see, sweetness?"

Adalyn practically melted to the floor. "*Jumanji.*"

"Sounds good to me."

"Oh, we definitely need new ones." A hint of jealousy was in Lake's voice.

"*Did they try to get* you to take them to the movies, too?" Vincent busted out laughing as he saw Nero enter the security room to watch the cameras.

"You fucking asshole. I know you told them to ask me." Nero threw himself down on the chair. "It was my fucking day off, too."

Vincent laughed even harder. "Don't bitch at me. You could have still had your day off if you had taken them."

"I can't handle them all by myself, you dick! Especially not with your crazy-ass sister. She rubs off on them too much. I can't even control Elle with her around."

"Sorry, unlike you, I actually had to work today." Hitting him on the shoulder, he told him his real plan. "And now I have you to keep me company."

Nero rubbed a hand through his black hair to keep from punching him in the face. "I swear to God, Vincent, one day, I'll fucking kill you if Lucca doesn't beat me to it first."

Vincent was unbothered. "You guys are just jealous because I'm smarter and better-looking than you."

Laughter came from the other side of the room, where Sal was on a high-tech computer, surrounded by monitors.

"The fact that you think that only makes me fucking want to kill you more." Nero had to get up and put distance between them so he wouldn't be tempted.

It's true. Vincent decided to admit it in his head instead of out loud this time.

Almost thirty minutes had passed when Sal spoke up while continuing to violently tap on his keyboard. "Nero, the coast is clear to go home, if you want."

"What do you mean?" Nero asked, turning around.

"The girls went to the movies, and Elle went with them."

Wasting no time, he stood up. "I'm out, then."

"Dammit!" Vincent felt defeated that his plan had failed. "Who took them?"

"Maria decided to join, so she has her men."

Nero stopped, worry etched on his face. "That's all they took? Two men isn't enough for all of them."

"Oh no, don't worry; Lucca told them that wasn't enough, so they got someone else."

"Okay, cool." Nero turned to leave again.

It wasn't adding up for Vincent. Who would have been left to take them? Everyone else was working. And those who weren't, were at home with their families.

"Who?" he asked.

"Angel," Sal answered while tapping away.

Nero stopped in his tracks. "Angel?"

"*Angel?*" Vincent stood up from his chair.

Sal finally turned around. "Yeah, that a problem?"

"Fuck yeah, it is," Vincent told him straight up. "I can't have him taking *my* girls to the movies. Lucca might trust him, but I sure as fuck don't."

Nero kept quiet, but by the look on his face, he didn't seem to like it either.

"He's making us look like assholes right now. Plus, you really trust him with Elle?" Vincent looked at Nero, already knowing the answer.

"Fuck," Nero cursed. "Did they leave already?"

"Yeah, about five minutes ag—"

"I'm going." His green eyes lit up fiercely.

"Fuck it, me, too." Vincent started to follow him, regardless if he was about to get denied. "Sal, can you cover for me? I'll owe you."

"You leaving is doing me a favor," Sal muttered.

"Jealousy..." He was starting to get really tired of everyone's shit. *It's not my fault I was blessed with this face.* "That's why you fuckers are ugly."

T*he girls just stood there,* watching Angel in awe as he went to get their movie tickets. Well, all of them except Maria.

Flipping her blonde locks behind her shoulder, she tried to reel them in. "If you three stare at him much longer, you're going to creep him the hell out."

"Yeah, you two already have men; quit staring at him like a piece of meat," Adalyn told them.

Elle finally turned her eyes away from him to look at her. "You stare at Nero like he is, and you don't hear me complain."

"Yeah, but you're nice, and Nero wouldn't ever leave you. See him?" Pointing at the sexy, tatted bad boy, she continued, "I would like to have him. It doesn't mean I'll get him, but I'd like to. And if by some freaking miracle God lets me have him, I'm definitely not going to be able to keep him if you two don't quit it!"

Maria practically snorted. "You're crazier than I thought if you think God wants you to be with him."

"Why not?" Sure, he was hot, bad, and maybe not the nicest person, but hell, that was exactly what she was looking for.

The blonde's eyes travelled all over him. "He's got about a hundred sins all over his body, and a one-way ticket to hell, I promise you that."

"Well, if so, I want to go with him," she breathed, thinking about all the sinful things she wanted to do with him.

"Mmhmm …" Lake and Elle cooed.

A cough right behind them had them turning around to see Nero and Vincent.

Elle looked like a deer in headlights. "What are you doing here?"

"Y-yeah, I thought you had to work?" Lake was just as surprised.

Vincent put on a great show. "We felt really bad for not being able to take you girls, so we asked Sal if he could cover for us."

"I bet you did." *If they believe that horseshit, I'll smack 'em.*

Angel came back with the tickets and passed them out to each girl. They couldn't help giving him a big smile with the sweetest "thank you" you had ever heard.

Nero grabbed Elle's waist, pulling her back to stand beside him.

Vincent also quickly snatched Lake by putting his arm around her and pulling her to his side. There seemed to be a bit of hastiness in his voice when he said, "Hey, man, we're gonna need two more."

Sliding the last ticket in his pocket, he didn't seem to care. "Then I'd go get them before they sell out."

Vincent started to see red, and Nero seemed to get a little pissed, too, as he leaned over and snatched up a ticket out of Todd, Maria's bodyguard's, hand.

Well, that was a little rude.

The pretty boy couldn't believe he was left to fend for himself, but then he found a ticket in his hand.

"I'll go get them." Maria had barely put them in his hand before she stormed off.

Her eyes didn't move as she glided across the floor. It was almost like an out-of-body experience. Her mind didn't catch up to what she was doing until their bodies hit each other.

His reflex was fast, turning around to catch and steady her. "Are you all right?"

"I'm so sorry. I must've not been paying attention." She acted surprised and a bit disoriented.

Looking back at Todd, who had followed her, she let him know she was all right. *Please stay put.*

"I think you're making this a bit of a habit." He laughed.

She let herself look up into his golden eyes. "Oh no, not you again. Now I feel awful."

"Don't." He continued to hold her up, not letting her go. "What's your name again? Maria, right?"

Smiling, she was happy that he remembered. "Yes. I'm sorry.

Remind me of yours—"

"Kayne Evans."

"That's right." It was hard to look away from him.

They both stared into the other's eyes for a few moments until he finally dropped his hands from her after realizing he hadn't let her go yet.

Clearing his throat, he moved up in the line. "What movie did you and your boyfriend come to see?"

"Huh?" Turning to see an intimidating Todd, she laughed. "Oh, he's not my boyfrie—"

"There you are!" A brunette came up to Kayne, smiling.

Kayne seemed off guard at first, like he hadn't expected her. "Hey, Kendra."

Adjusting her fur coat, Maria quickly realized they were here to see a movie together.

A moment of awkward silence passed between them.

"Kendra, this is Maria."

"Is she one of your students?" the brunette asked.

"No," he corrected her before a corner of his mouth slightly lifted. "We just seem to run into each other."

"Yes, we do." Maria chuckled.

It's strange, she thought as she looked at the sexy golden man.

She almost forgot about the woman standing beside him, too enthralled at the spark she felt between them. It was why she had run into him again, but this time on purpose. She had wanted to see if she felt that again. Never having it before with any other person, she had missed it, dreamt about it nightly, almost forgetting what it had felt like until she saw his silhouette at the back of the line. That was when she had found herself running into him, wanting to see if she could get that feeling back.

"I think it's our turn," Kendra interrupted their staring.

"Right. Well, it was good seeing you again, Maria, and hopefully, I'll run into you sometime again," he ended with another smile.

"Hopefully," she wished, watching him walk away with his hand at the small of the woman's back.

That was when she felt it. A twitch … in her cold … dead … heart.

Watching Maria walk away so quickly, Adalyn found it odd that she would so willingly give up her ticket to get one for herself, but she wasn't able to put much thought into it because of the escalading feelings going on around her.

"Do you want some popcorn?" Angel asked her.

"I do." Lake smiled.

So did Elle. "Me, too."

The boys clearly didn't like the girls' responses, so they each pushed their women along to the popcorn and candy stand. However, Vincent was the one who threw Angel a hot glance. "We got this. Come on, Adalyn."

She didn't know what he expected, but she didn't move as she watched the back of him get smaller. She figured he was going to be really surprised when he found out she hadn't followed him like a good little sister.

Looking up at Angel, she couldn't help laughing. "I don't think they like you very much, especially my brother."

"That one's your brother?" he asked, shocked, as he watched Vincent drag Lake along.

"Yep."

"You two look nothing alike."

You mean, he's ridiculously good-looking and I'm not?

"That's because we're stepbrother and sister."

Putting a hand on her arm to lead her toward the popcorn stand, he mumbled under his breath, "Well, that's good."

"Huh?" Unable to hear with all the people, she'd missed what he had said.

"Do you want butter on your popcorn?"

"Oh yes, please."

As they waited in one of the many lines, she couldn't help feeling as if the longer she stood there, the more uncomfortable she became. Looking around for the source of her discomfort, her eyes landed on three tattooed males wearing grungy suits.

Instantly, her heart knew. *Lucianos.*

With her mouth dry from their intense staring, the words finally managed to come out, "Are they . . .?"

"Yes," he answered her quickly and quietly without even turning his head to look at them. Pulling her to stand beside him, he blocked her from their view and their view of her. "Stop staring at them, sweetness."

She snapped her head to the front, not needing to be told twice. Adalyn wasn't sure if he told her that because her staring might piss them off, but she wasn't eager to find out.

Catching her nerves, he tried to calm her. "They're not going to hurt you as long as you keep your eyes to yourself."

Welp, that answered that.

Something about this felt strange to her. She couldn't ever remember seeing a Luciano before while she was out. If she had, they at least hadn't made it obvious who they were. So, why now? Especially with it being the first time Angel and she went somewhere besides school.

"How come I've never seen a Luciano out before?"

"You're only seeing them because they are checking to see if I'm okay and that the Carusos are holding up their end of the deal."

"Oh." Licking her lips, she supposed that should make her feel better. "So, that's good, then, that they see you're fine and alive?"

"Not exactly." He took a step forward in line, maintaining his calm expression. "They see me with a Caruso girl, about to enjoy a movie. They're looking at me how they look at Carusos."

Every hair on her body stood up from his words. If they looked at him that way, one of Lucifer's sons, that wasn't good.

"Should you go talk to them?"

"No," was all he said as he stepped up to the counter to order. Thankfully, it was quick, and by the time they got their stuff, the rest of their group had found them.

Vincent, Nero, and Maria's harsh expression told them they

knew the other Lucianos were there.

"Let's go," Vincent said, this time putting an arm around both Lake and her.

Don't look, don't look, don't look.

Her blood ran cold as they passed the Lucianos on their way into the movie theater.

Shit, I'm gonna look.

She had set out to only give a quick glance, but she just couldn't look away.

Who seemed to be the youngest Luciano stood in the middle and smiled evilly at her, revealing a golden grill that was faceted in diamonds.

Again, she couldn't explain it, and she didn't know how she knew, but one thing was for certain. That golden smile of death was for her and her alone.

HELLEVATOR

Holding the elevator doors open once it reached the penthouse floor, Angel let everyone get off first. When Adalyn came out last, he said, "I can take you home whenever you're ready. Just knock on my door."

She hesitated, looking at Lake, who was quietly telling her to go on. It didn't take her a second to get back on the elevator, not wanting to leave Angel just yet. "It's pretty late. We should go now."

"Actually, I'll take you." Vincent moved to get back on the elevator, but Lake held his hand tightly.

"No, I need you."

"What for?" he asked sharply, more focused on Angel taking his sister home. But when Lake whispered in his ear and started to drag them toward their room, Vincent no longer fought her.

"Bye!" Adalyn laughed, waving at her now distracted brother

while the door started to close.

Okay, maybe Lake dating my brother isn't so bad after all.

With the door closed, and her and Angel alone, she watched the numbers start to tick down. There was something different between them now. He hadn't been obligated to go out with her, nor was she just a job today. It had changed things and almost turned their relationship on its head, making her wonder if he had gone only to get the ring back or because he might actually enjoy her company.

All she had to do was ... find out.

Unable to keep from smiling, she continued to watch the numbers tick down. "Thank you for coming with us. I had a great time tonight."

"I di—"

Adalyn shrieked as the elevator went dark and came to an abrupt stop. When she fell into Angel's arms from the jolt, he caught her and held on. Scared shitless, she wasn't about to let him go.

"What the hell happened?"

"I have no fucking clue." Holding on to her in case it started working again, he hit some buttons, but it was pointless. It seemed like no power was getting to the elevator.

He pulled out his cell phone and quickly called a number before putting it to his ear. It rang only a couple of times.

"Lucca, can you hear me? Lucca ...? We're stuck in the elevat—" Hanging up the phone, he cursed, "Shit."

"Oh God. What is it?"

"There was too much static on the other end. I couldn't hear him. I'm not sure what happened."

She shakily pulled out her phone, trying to send a text message to Vincent, but it wasn't going through.

Oh, shit. Oh, shit. Oh, shit.

"Oh, shit. Oh, shit. Oh, shit."

"Everything will be fine, Adalyn." He gave her arms a tight squeeze, trying to make her focus on him. "I think the power has just gone out in the hotel. It should come back on soon."

She took a long, deep breath, trying to calm her nerves. Taking a look around the tight, dark box they were in, however, she only hoped he was right. It isn't until you're stuck in a suspended elevator that you realize you might have had a fear of it all along.

"Sit down, sweetness." Angel helped her down to the floor to help her feel more grounded.

They sat there for several minutes in silence, just waiting for the elevator to start moving again. With each passing minute, the space became smaller. By the time thirty minutes had passed with no movement or help from the outside world, she did the only thing she could do at this point. She put her head down and quickly touched her forehead, chest, and each shoulder, making the sign of the cross.

Dear Lord, this is not what I fucking asked for when I wanted to spend more time with Angel. No man is worth this shi—

"What are you doing?"

"Praying to our Lord and Savior to not let this elevator fall fifteen stories to our death."

Laughing, Angel wrapped an arm around the back of her

shoulders. "I promise you, sweetness, everything will be all right."

"How in the hell are you so calm right now?" She pressed into him, wondering what type of other sick shit he must enjoy since *this* clearly wasn't affecting him. The walls looked like they were practically closing in on her, although she knew they were solid, immovable objects.

Shrugging, nothing seemed to faze him. "You have to remember I've been sitting in a tiny-ass hotel room for a while now."

"Really?"

"I've sorta been a prisoner, sweetness," he reminded her.

"Wow." She looked over at him, fully realizing the depth of his situation and how he must have felt if this situation didn't seem so bad to him. "Dealing with this family and being away from yours, then having to deal with me … I'm sorry. This must all be pretty shitty for you."

"You're not so bad. I can't say the same about the rest …" When he finished his sentence, it held a different tone, "but I'll survive."

Seeing the determination in his dark depths was when she noticed something about him for the first time. His presence held something reminiscent of Chloe's. Every time she looked at the scarred girl, one word came to her mind. And right now, in this moment, looking at Angel, that word came to her again. *Survivor.*

She didn't know his story, and she didn't think a man like him would ever trust anyone enough to tell it, especially to a Caruso girl, but maybe, just maybe, he might let her in enough to learn something.

"Do you miss them?"

It took him a while to answer.

"Yes," he finally admitted to the tiny space they shared.

"Well, I hope you get to go home soon." Her words came out a bit raspy.

They had been hard for her to say, not knowing if it was because she didn't want him to leave just yet or because that was exactly what she wanted for herself—to go home and get out of this elevator. The longer she was stuck in there, the more she felt like she was suffocating and running out of air.

Angel reached into his jean pocket and pulled out a piece of candy that was wrapped tightly in a wrapper. "Suck on this and try not to chew it. I have a few more pieces, if it helps."

"You keep candy on you?" she asked, finding it strange. That was something just women usually kept in their purse.

Shrugging, he answered simply, "Habit."

Unwrapping the sweet candy and putting it in her mouth, she found it weirdly helped, even if it was just a little. As she let the juices flow into her mouth, she wondered how he knew it would help. She only wished it would start the elevator again, as the metal box was starting to get chilly.

"I don't know how much longer I'm gonna last in here, Angel." As her chest rose up and down, the space started to feel even smaller. "This is really starting to freak me the fuc—"

He crashed his lips down on hers hard and fast, making her instantly forget about being stuck. She supposed that had been his goal, but she damn sure was going to take what she could get and milk it for all it was worth.

This kiss was exactly what she had been expecting from him. He was demanding, rough, and shameless, making her open her mouth to him. She gratefully did so, letting his tongue enter to play with hers. Her chilly body was instantly heated from the inside out, making her feel like she was about to burn alive.

Angel knew exactly what he was doing to her. Searching her mouth, he captured the little piece of sweet candy she hadn't sucked all the way yet and took it into his, stealing it.

Having the candy stolen with a sensual flick of his tongue, she now tasted the cherry sweetness in his hot mouth. Unable to help it, she moaned, which echoed in the metal box, heightening the experience.

Trying to get closer to him, Adalyn wanted more. Badly.

He helped her out, moving her to straddle his lap to give them both easier access.

Oh God. The elevator falling was the least of her worries now.

Letting her tongue slide into his mouth, she searched for the candy, mimicking what he had done by flicking her tongue and capturing it. He wasn't going to let it go easily, though. But before he went to take it back, she playfully nipped his tongue, making him pull away.

Smiling down at him, she finally bit the candy. "I won."

Not even a second passed before he flipped her onto her back, and his hard body hovered over her. "You bit me, sweetness." Her grabbed her chin, his heated eyes boring into hers. "That wasn't very smart."

Holding her breath, she felt every muscle go taut.

"I could take you right here"—he slid his inked hand to her throat, giving it a light squeeze—"and no one could stop me." Sliding his hand down, he started unbuttoning her coat, slowly reaching for each one, revealing the light sweater underneath. "No one could hear you moan," he continued as he went up the warm material and spanned his cold hand over her lower belly. "Or scream."

She melted beneath him; that was exactly what her fucked-up self wanted. But, like always, he knew it.

"Is that what you want?" He moved his hand up, sliding over her tiny waist and ribs, placing it right under her breasts.

Fuck yes.

She only managed to nod.

With his inked hand, he went under the thin, lacy material, cupping her right breast. Her tanned nipples got even harder under his grasp.

"Say it, then," he demanded harshly.

"Y-yes!" she cried when he rubbed her nipple between his fingers.

He then freed his hand from her breast, only to move to the waistband of her jeans. She swallowed hard when he unbuttoned the top button, exposing the rim of her silky black panties.

Moving his lips centimeters from hers, he gave her one last warning, ready to slide his fingertips down from where they rested steadily under the silk. "You sure about that, sweetness?"

Taking one final breath, not knowing if she would regret it until it was too late, she raised her mouth up to meet his, giving her answer by taking another bite of him and pulling on his bottom lip.

He was fast, sliding his long fingers inside her, forcing her to quickly release his lip on the loud moan that escaped her.

She was wet, hot, and ready, only making it easier for the taking. The only bit of trouble he had was her tightness.

Adalyn thought she was seeing stars from feeling him inside her. She spread her legs as much as she could to try to help him make it feel better, but it was just such a tight fit.

Seeing her distress, he slowed his fingers down, moving them in and out of her slick pussy a centimeter at a time. "How is it that you're still a virgin when you've been practically begging me to fuck you?"

It wasn't really a question but a statement, since Adalyn had never made it a secret when she was attracted to a man. And with her taste in them, it was a wonder how she had been able to stay a virgin so long. With her head in the clouds, however, the only thing that came out of her mouth was her hot, heavy breaths.

This time when Angel inched his finger out, he slid in one more, stretching her walls. She almost screamed out in pain this time, but then he placed his thumb on her sensitive clit, turning it into pleasure.

He made no effort to hide from her, showing her exactly who and what kind of lover he was. There was no pretending, no sweetness, no purity. Instead, it was demanding, rough, and sinful … but oh so wickedly pleasurable.

Adalyn held his shoulders, feeling the fire burn deep inside her with every flick of his expert thumb and sunken fingers, but he never let her burn, only throwing more gasoline on the fire.

"Please ..." she whimpered.

"Do you wanna come, sweetness?" he whispered into her ear with a rough voice.

Wiggling her hips, she tried to do it herself, but he still wouldn't let her, toying with her like she was putty in his hands.

"Yes, please!"

Angel gave her another hard kiss, paying attention to her heavy bottom lip before biting the sensitive flesh. Then he pulled his fingers out of her and slid his hand out of her jeans.

Giving her a twisted smile, he stared down at her and gave her one final warning, "You can't win, Adalyn. I'll win every time."

When her mouth dropped open, the elevator's lights turned on and the ground beneath them started to move.

He got up from on top of her, standing in one quick movement.

What the—

Looking up at numbers that were dinging above the elevator door, she watched them get higher and higher, taking them to the top.

Not having time to think, she quickly buttoned her jeans before standing, then started buttoning her coat back up while Angel lazily stood there with a smirk on his face.

It was all a blur. She didn't even know if that had really happened.

Did I just ...?

Did he just ...?

The look on his face and the fire still burning inside her told her it really fucking had.

"You assho—"

The elevator doors slid open, revealing Lucca standing there, patiently waiting.

Oh fuck.

The shock, horror, and embarrassment on her face were enough to make her wish for the elevator to fall over twenty stories to her death.

"There was a city blackout," Lucca revealed as he blocked the doors from closing, not moving to let them exit the hellevator.

Swallowing loudly, she didn't know what to say when Angel just nodded.

Lucca's demon eyes moved between them for several moments.

"Adalyn, go stay with Lake tonight."

At his command, she wasted no time, jumping out of the elevator and sliding past him. "Okay."

"Angel, follow me."

She stopped in her tracks, turning to watch Lucca head toward his office.

When Angel passed her, crossing the elevator threshold, she didn't see a man who was scared, worried, or regretful. She saw a man who was pleased.

Taking two of his long, tatted fingers, he placed them in his mouth, licking the ones that had been deep inside her, before he walked away, giving her his back.

She tilted her head to the side, replaying that look on his face when he had licked them to taste her. *God ... damn.*

*S*taring down at the *lifeless* body, he stood there just as motionless until his younger brother squatted to touch the single bullet that had gone right between the eyes.

"It's clean, just how Lucca described it with his man. No wonder he said you could've done it." Matthias rubbed the blood between his fingers after touching the bullet wound.

When his brother didn't answer, he looked up. "Dominic?"

"Check his body," he demanded after another moment of thought.

Matthias began searching his body, finding the young Luciano to be in perfect condition everywhere else. Standing up, he waited for further instruction.

"Get Lucca on the phone," Dominic hissed before squatting himself to examine the body closer.

Something wasn't right about this. He could feel it in his gut in the pavement beneath his shoes. A soft rumbling that was about to shake this city to its very core, and soon, everything would come crumbling down.

Putting his fingers to the cold, purple lips, he parted them, revealing a diamond and gold grill that was still perfectly in place.

That rumbling beneath him seemed to vibrate closer to the surface. *It's coming,* a war between the two oldest families in this city that had dueled since its conception. A war that had been easily won by the Carusos in the past, but this time, it would be different, because of two men alone.

Lucca Caruso.

And Dominic Luciano.

Two kings in one city. A city that would fall this time, as both men were kings and each one would rather see it fall than have the other win.

I'm just waiting for the perfect moment.

Angel sat down across from Lucca, not worried in the slightest. The cameras hadn't been working in the elevator, and unless she opened her mouth, Lucca wouldn't be able to prove shit.

A hidden smile appeared behind his eyes at the thought of Adalyn having to retell the story of what he had just done to her in the elevator. He would bet a million dollars that she wouldn't be able to bring herself to tell it.

Neither family would know what had happened in that elevator tonight. He would make sure.

Continuing to stare at the demon, he wasn't sure what Lucca was going to say, but the last thing he had expected was what did come out of his mouth.

"Andre is dead."

"What?" Angel shook his head, trying to grasp the words.

Flicking his Zippo open, Lucca lit a cigarette. "Dominic found him during the blackout with the same bullet hole Tom had between his eyes."

This wasn't good. Someone was really trying to start a war between the families, and just like Tom, he had probably been one of the last people to see him alive.

Not knowing if he wanted to share the information with Lucca, he asked, "May I have permission to see my family and pay my respects?"

Lucca stared at him hard for a moment before speaking with finality, "No."

Angel should have known Lucca wouldn't let him, not with this shitstorm brewing between them.

"Is that it, then?"

Giving a quick nod, Lucca dismissed him. Before Angel could leave, though, Lucca decided to give him some advice.

"I'd be very careful with Adalyn if I were you."

Lying came easy to him. "I haven't done anyth—"

"I think you've misunderstood." Lucca inhaled deeply as he took a drag. "You're the one who should be worried of her."

Something told Angel he should question Lucca about her, but he didn't. Instead, he closed the door behind him, going against his instincts. There was no match between him and Adalyn. Just like he had told her in the elevator … *I'll win every time.*

Ding.

Once he reached his hotel room, Angel pulled his phone out of his pocket. A voicemail had been left, and before he even heard the sweet, saddened voice come through the phone, his stomach sank.

"Angel …? It's Andre. He's … I just need to see you."

Throwing his phone across the room, Angel smashed it against the wall, the walls that were holding him here, away from his family, away from her.

He took several deep breaths before reaching into his pocket, pulling out a piece of candy, and popping it into his mouth. Closing his eyes, he focused on …

…The cherry flavor had almost completely dissipated in his mouth from the third one Dominic had brought him. His mouth now felt drier than ever.

He held himself tightly, silently rocking himself back and forth, feeling his mind start to slip into the dark, dark abyss.

Reaching the end, Angel had sadly run out of time …

The sound of the lock sliding out of place, followed by light pouring into the tiny closet, had him slamming his eyes shut and covering them with his little hands. It was almost as if the sun itself was in the space.

Squinting, he looked up to see the devil's wretched face staring down at him. It was a look he would never forget for as long as he lived. A look of pure fury. That was when he knew he had won.

"Clean this shit up," Lucifer hissed at Dominic, who was standing in the doorway, before he turned and left.

Closing his eyes again, he felt a hand touch his forehead.

"You did good, Angel."

Angel didn't bother opening his eyes as he asked, "D-did I-I?"

"You did." Taking his arm, Dominic slowly tried to raise him. "Now, let's clean you up."

The embarrassment of soiling himself several times made him not want to get up, but his brother wouldn't have it, forcing him to try.

Angel couldn't even move at first, yet he eventually got himself up enough to lean on Dominic for support. Each step hurt and felt foreign.

Stopping halfway to the bathroom, he didn't know how much longer he could walk, until his eyes drifted into his bedroom, seeing Matthias curled up on his bed.

Angel was looking at someone who looked like his brother yet was no longer.

Falling to his knees, he wanted it all to just end.

Dominic sat down beside him, his eyes going between his twin brothers. "Bella asked me today where you and Matthias are."

"S-she did?" Something deep down inside him lit up.

"Yes, I think she misses you."

That thing deep down in him . . . stirred as he pushed himself up off the ground to stand tall. Taking a step. . .

…Angel walked over to his fallen phone, picking it back up. As he looked down at the cracked screen, his finger hovered over Matthias's name before pushing call.

"Yes, brother?" his twin asked.

Smiling, he had just one question for him.

"Heads or tails?"

Sneaking out of Vincent and Lake's place the next day, Adalyn started the journey to the elevator, wondering if she really should do this. When she hit the button, she decided not to turn back, even when she walked down the hall and knocked on the door that she now stood in front of.

When the door was opened, revealing Angel, there seemed to be something . . . off.

Crossing his arms, he leaned against the doorframe while unashamedly travelling his eyes all up and down her body.

She started to feel self-conscious from his blatant staring, which made her severely regret coming to see him. If she had known he would act like this after the elevator ride from hell, she wouldn't have come.

Clearing her throat, she came out with it. "After what you said yesterday, I felt bad about you being stuck here all day." When he didn't speak, she continued, "I thought maybe we could do something that didn't involve you being my babysitter, if you wanted."

"Adalyn." A smile finally touched his lips that lit up his eyes. "Wow, you're awfully pretty … today."

Confused, she glanced down at herself. "I slept over at Lake's, so I literally look the same as yesterday." *Wait … Did he just call me pretty?*

"Right, I know that." Reaching out, he grabbed a lock of her thick brown hair. "So, what do you have in mind, sweetness?"

With that dark look in his eyes, she didn't think they were on the same page. She *did* want to go into his hotel room and have him properly finish what he had started yesterday, but the cameras were on today, and she would be damned if she would let him do that to her again.

"You're the one who's been stuck in here. What do you wanna do?"

Wrapping her hair around his finger, he gave it a light tug. "Oh, I can think of several things we can do."

Heat rushed to her cheeks, not knowing where this Angel had fallen from, but holy fuck, if she didn't think of something quick, she wouldn't give a shit who saw her walk into his room.

Trying to think fast, she saw the skateboard he had stolen out of the corner of her eye. *Oh yes.*

She smiled from ear to ear. "I have an idea."

His brow raised. "What's that?"

"Show me what you can do on that skateboard."

Angel smiled, not taking a second to answer, "Sure thing, sweetness."

She watched him turn around to quickly throw on a sweatshirt, then he grabbed the board and closed the door behind them.

"Let's go." He threw his free arm around her, pulling her down the hall.

Adalyn laughed at his sudden enthusiasm. "Where are we going? The elevator's the other way."

"We're taking the stairs today."

"That's probably a good idea after last night," she agreed; thankfully, they were only nine floors up.

He looked over at her strangely for a moment but continued walking.

"What did Lucca say to you?" she whispered. "Do you think he knows what happened in the elevator?"

Opening the door for the stairs for her, he grinned. "Oh no, we just talked about family stuff."

She stopped, staring at him for a second. *Wasn't his tattoo on the . . .?*

Shaking her head, she went through the door, and then they headed down the steps, going through the casino and out to the parking garage.

"This'll do." He smiled before he tossed his board down and jumped on.

Adalyn's mouth fell open at the speed he took off in. Her head moved around and around as she watched him weave through the huge parking garage. When he jumped midair, spinning the board with his feet, she almost passed the fuck out. *No way in hell is Lake ever seeing him do this.*

Heading straight toward her, Angel turned his board at the last second and began riding around her in circles. "Wanna learn how to ride, sweetness?"

It was hard for her to think while watching the sexy bad boy spin around her. "I don't ... I don't think I can."

"Sure you can." He got off, coming up behind her and grabbing her by the waist. Leaning down, he whispered in her ear, "I'll help you."

Adalyn didn't have to be told twice. She placed a foot on the skateboard and lightly pushed with her other to get it to move. Wobbling and falling off every second, she was thankful Angel held her steady. She tried again and again, but even with the baby increments, she couldn't stop falling off, making her die of laughter.

"I think I'm helpless here."

Finding it funny, too, he held her waist tighter. "Nah, I got all day to teach you."

She continued to have the best time with him as he helplessly taught her how to ride a skateboard. After about an hour, she had graduated to being able to only hold his hand while she glided the board on the concrete beneath her. However, as she hit her first rock while laughing so hard, she almost flew straight off the board. Angel's sharp reflexes, though, had him catching her.

"Whoa, sweetness." He held her tightly, moving his face closer to hers. "I think I deserve something for saving your life."

Staring up at him, she bit her bottom lip. "What do you want?"

When his lips touched hers, she should have been prepared, knowing full well it had been coming, yet she still hadn't anticipated it.

This kiss was different than the rest he had given her, not rough or demanding like the others but sensual and precise as he smoothed his tongue over her bottom lip where she had bitten it. It might have not been what she had expected, but it sure was equally as sexy. She almost couldn't believe that it was Angel until she opened her eyes again.

"That's a start," he told her with a grin.

Adalyn laughed at him. "That's a start? What else do you want?"

"I thought you might give me the ring back, since I saved your life and all."

"Oh, now I see why you've been so nice to me today." Wiggling out of his arms, she wasn't going to let him know it might be working.

Taking her hand, he pulled her close again. "Come on, sweetness; I'll let you have a lot more than a kiss if you give it ba—"

"No, you won't," a low voice spoke from behind them.

Nothing in this world would have ever prepared her for what she saw when she turned around.

Adalyn opened her mouth to scream, but a tatted hand covered it before a sound could escape.

What the . . .? While she continued to scream into his hand, her eyes flew back and forth.

They landed on the one who she had just been skateboarding with. *Angel?*

Then she looked at the hooded one. *And Angel?*

"I take it you didn't tell her you had a twin." Angel number one or two, or whoever the fuck wasn't holding her mouth, said.

She screamed even louder. *A twin!*

The hooded Angel held her mouth tighter, trying to dampen

the sound. "Obviously not, fucker, or you wouldn't have gotten this far with her."

Non-hooded Angel's smile quickly turned to concern. "She's gonna pass out if you don't get her to stop."

"Adalyn, calm the hell down!" Angel with a hood whispered harshly.

Stopping suddenly, she came to the realization that the hooded one was the Angel she knew.

The second he pulled his hand from her mouth, she tried her best to keep her voice down as she asked, "Who the fuck is he? And why does he look like you?"

"Wow, that was fast." Angel whoever-the-hell laughed from her instantly knowing *which* Angel was *her* Angel.

"This is Matthias, my twin brother," Angel said as if it weren't obvious enough.

Holy mother of God . . . I'll be Goddamned.

Unable to stop looking between the two identical beings in front of her, she looked at their tattoos that were all matching but flipped, on opposite sides. She supposed she should have known that wasn't Angel, but then again, what fucking twins get matching tattoos all over their body?

Speechless, nothing but stammering came out of her mouth.

"Maybe you should have continued to let her believe I was you."

"I would have if you weren't trying to fuck her," Angel snapped.

Matthias rolled his eyes over her. "I think she liked me better. I might still have a sho—"

"Get the fuck out of here before someone else finding us both will be better than what I'll do to you." Threatening him, he shot him a final warning glance.

"Fine," Matthias sighed before looking straight into Adalyn's brown depths. "I thought we might be able to share her this time, but I can't say I blame you."

Share . . . me? Dear God . . .

She would be willing to die and go to heaven for a chanc—

Angel grabbed her chin, forcing her to look away from Matthias and up at him. "You ever kiss him again, I won't believe you didn't know it was me."

Swallowing, she nodded in understanding.

"Did you like him better?" He continued to stare at her, ready to detect a lie.

She quickly shook her head.

"Good." He flipped up the skateboard, catching it in his hand. "I didn't wanna have to kill him."

PAMELA ANDERSON CIRCA BAYWATCH

"**U**m, why exactly was your brother pretending to be you yesterday?" Adalyn asked when they were almost to the school. She'd had the night to think about what had happened yesterday, and seeing him have a freaking twin distracted her from that.

Angel slightly paused in thought while driving, seeming to debate what to tell her before he spoke. "A Luciano died the night we got stuck in the elevator."

Her skin went cold. "What?"

"One of the guys who came to see me at the movies was killed the same way Tom was."

She bit her lip in nervousness. Something in her already knew who it was, but she had to ask.

"W-which one?"

"The one who stood in the middle. He had the grill."

Holy shit. Whatever was happening between the families wasn't good, and it definitely wasn't good for whatever the hell was happening between her and Angel.

Swallowing hard, she tried not to think about it too much. "So, you two switched—"

"Because I needed to talk to the family," he finished for her, putting the car in park.

Getting out of the car, the two joined the group, only to see Vincent standing beside Lake.

"Uh, why are you here?" Adalyn asked, confused.

Lake stared at her shoes, looking like a puppy that had just done something bad.

"Since Tom's death, Lucca needed a replacement." His baby blues looked straight at Angel. "I volunteered because, who best to watch my girl and my sister than me?"

Adalyn blinked repeatedly as Vincent put his arm around Lake and started walking her to class. *Poor Lake.*

Angel was completely unbothered and looked like he had just been swatted at by a kitten.

"He does realize that it's very hard to find a guy as pretty as him threatening, right?"

She went to open her mouth, but then decided to close it to keep that information about her brother to herself. *It'll be a fun surprise.*

They headed to the classroom; Lake and Vincent waited at the door for them, but when the girls walked in and Angel went to follow behind, her brother looked confused.

"What are you doing?"

"I watch them from inside the classroom," Angel told him.

Putting his hand on his shoulder, Vincent stopped him. "We're supposed to wait outside and watch the door."

Angel stared down at his hand, looking like he was about to punch him. To Adalyn's surprise, though, he seemed to change tactics.

"See this classroom?" He pointed to the full classroom of over a hundred students who were half asleep. "Any one of them could be a murderer, or worse, try to flirt with your girl. We have to assume everyone's a threat, so I sit right behind them all the way in the back, where I can keep an eye on everyone."

The pretty boy's mind seemed to be blown. "Good call."

Rolling his eyes when Vincent headed into the classroom with Lake, he mumbled under his breath, "He's not very smart, is he?"

That, Adalyn agreed with. "Nope. He's not."

Taking her seat next to Lake, she was ready to whisper so the boys couldn't hear, when her friend beat her to the punch.

"He's mad at me," Lake came out with it.

Adalyn started to laugh, knowing exactly where this was going.

"He said I was staring at him too much, and that it looked like I had the hots for Angel. I think even Elle got in trouble with Nero, because I heard Vincent on the phone with him, promising that he'd keep an eye on Elle around him, too."

"Well, what did you say?" Trying to hold her laughter back was almost impossible.

"I asked him if he would have the hots for Pamela Anderson circa *Baywatch* if she was around him."

If Adalyn had had water in her mouth, she would have choked.

Lake sank lower in her seat, realizing that maybe comparing Angel's looks to quite possibly one of the biggest sex symbols ever hadn't been the best idea. "And that's why he's here."

"I'd say so." Adalyn chuckled at her friend.

Thank God, I didn't tell her he can ride a skateboard. There really wouldn't have been a chance for her to be with Angel if she had.

This class and the next one were spent with Lake sure to divert her eyes from staring too deeply at Angel. By the time lunch came around, Adalyn was proud Lake had made it this far without even one forbidden glance while her boyfriend wasn't looking. One thing was for sure, she deserved a medal because he had looked especially hot to her today, now that most of his bruising had lightened up.

All of them decided to eat in the cafeteria today since fries were on the menu. Even Angel, who didn't usually eat on the job, got some.

Taking a seat beside Lake, their table had changed up a bit since Vincent now sat with them.

Maria's eyes followed Angel, who started to head to his normal table a few feet away. "Angel? Sit with us." She pointed with her fork to the empty chair beside Adalyn.

They all stopped at the fact that she wanted to include him. And this time, Adalyn literally did choke on her water.

Did Maria Caruso really just invite a Luciano to sit with her?

He seemed to be slightly stunned himself before setting his tray down on the table.

Holy shit, she did.

Looking over at Maria, then at Angel, who now sat beside her, she realized it was a monumental moment that brought inexplicable joy to her heart. To get the mafia princess, who was born without a heart, to like the son of Lucifer meant that, maybe someday, the two families could actually get along.

Even Lake and Elle were smiling at Maria's generosity. Well, at least until a scary look appeared in Vincent's eye. He was making it obvious that he wasn't so thrilled about her invitation.

"Since when have you wanted to be within five feet of a Luciano?" Vincent decided to call her out.

Flipping her hair behind her shoulder, she gave the pretty boy a deadly smile. "Since you started feeling threatened by one."

Oh.

My.

God.

Shocked faces around the table waited to see what Vincent would do.

He just picked up his food and started eating. There was nothing he could say. It was almost like watching a lion bow to a lioness.

Leave it to Maria to put any man in his place. She was a true inspiration.

The awkwardness at the table slowly faded the longer they sat there, with the girls doing most of the talking. Angel didn't speak while he lazily sat there, eating beside her, which was fine by her as she reached over and stole a couple of his fries. By about the fifth one, however, he finally did.

Speaking in a low tone, he said, "Steal another fry, sweetness, and you'll regret it."

Adalyn smiled sweetly at him while she reached over, stealing one last fry. "You can't do anything with my brother here." Popping it into her mouth when he didn't stop her, she felt her smile get bigger. She stole a couple of extra fries before they started to leave just for good measure.

Ha. That's right.

With lunch over, they all got up to deposit their trays, but Vincent had taken Lake's from her, getting rid of it himself.

Angel grabbed Adalyn's from her, too, making her blush slightly, but when he leaned down to whisper to Lake, her face went red for a different reason.

"Adalyn lied. I do know how to skateboard."

I WANT YOUR
BROTHER'S NUMBER

Watching Lake walk up ahead beside Vincent, Adalyn snapped her eyes to Angel. "If you tell her you know how to ride a motorcycle … I want your brother's number."

She had watched Lake officially give up on not looking at him after he had told her he could skate. Even Vincent, who was practically running her away from Angel to the safety of the Escalade, had given up hope that she would keep her eyes to herself. It was hard for Adalyn to blame her, but she could blame Angel for telling her the truth, which she clearly couldn't handle.

He put his arm around her, not caring if Vincent decided to look back. "Not a chance in hell, sweetness."

Adalyn couldn't help laughing. It was good to know she could always threaten him with Matthias if she needed.

Continuing to walk to the car, they tried their best to keep up with the couple in front of them until they saw the asshole skater with his friends coming right at them. Then they picked up their speed, trying to catch up to Lake and Vincent before they got to them.

"Today's the day, bitch." The skater's voice was loud and angry, getting louder and louder the closer he got. "I want my board back, and I'm going to steal your bitch, too, when we're through with you."

"Vincent!" Lake yelled when he let go of her hand and started raising his fist. "You promised you would stop getting into figh—"

Vincent sent the prick flying to the concrete, knocking him out cold in one precise punch to the face. The sound of the skater hitting the ground had his friends freezing in place before they all slowly backed away, seeing the crazed look in Vincent's baby blue eyes.

"Goddammit." Lake just shook her head as Vincent took her hand again and they stepped over the lifeless body.

Adalyn and Angel stared down at the skater for several moments in silence. When she finally looked at Angel, she could see it written on the bad boy's face—he had severely misjudged Vincent, not seeing the split personality and certifiable craziness.

Nodding, he wrapped an arm around Adalyn again, seeming to approve Vincent's not-so-pretty-boy side. "That works for me."

I knew it'd be more fun to let him find out on his own.

"Hey, lovebirds." Maria's voice sounded from behind them as she also headed toward the car with her bodyguards.

Her comment didn't stop Angel from keeping his arm

around Adalyn.

"There's a surprise party tonight for Vincent's dad's birthday. We're having it at my house. Everyone's invited." Maria started to pass them. Even in her stilettos, her long legs took her places. She looked back and raised a manicured brow. "That includes you, Luciano."

Adalyn narrowed her eyes at Maria as the blonde walked away. She knew she had seen something behind Maria's eyes that told Adalyn the mafia princess was up to something. She didn't know what it was yet, but she did know Angel going to the consigliere's birthday would get the blonde what she wanted.

Not knowing how she felt about him going into a lion's den full of Carusos alone, she prayed his answer would be no when she asked, "You're not going, are you?"

His gray depths told her there was something in it for him as well. "You never turn down a good party, sweetness."

"What are you doing here?" Lucca came over to Vincent and Nero. "I told you that you're banned from my home."

"It's my fucking dad's birthday; you expected me not to come?" Vincent looked at him like he was crazy.

"Yes," Lucca said coldly.

"Come on, Lucca; I've told you my face just looks like thi—"

"Then keep that fuckin' face away from Chloe." The underboss didn't let him finish.

Nero shook his head at his friend when he looked to him for help. "Dumbass, I've told you a thousand times that's not an excuse."

He rolled his eyes, then they landed on a tatted body. "What the fuck is *he* doing here?"

"Unlike you, he was invited," Lucca spat.

Vincent couldn't believe it. "You mean, you invited him over *me?*"

"Yes." Lucca's response was harsh as he looked for Chloe, seeing her talking to Maria and Leo in the corner of the room.

Both boys knew why he had done it—to see if Angel distressed her. However, she hadn't seemed to notice him walk in.

Throwing back the water in his cup, Vincent wished it was hard liquor as he watched Angel walk up to a welcoming Adalyn, Lake, and Elle. "I hate him."

Turning back to the pretty boy, the underboss was interested in what he had to say. "Why?"

He almost couldn't get the heinous words out. "Because I think he might be better-looking than me."

Lucca looked at Nero before leaving to go to Chloe's side. "Keep him the fuck away from me."

DEAD AND GONE

The party had been going just fine. Maybe she had been worried for no reason?

I'm sure Lucca put the fear of God into every Caruso here not to touch Angel in any way.

It was reaching the end of the party when the front door was opened and Amo walked into the room.

It had been a while since Adalyn had seen him last. Every time she had asked about him, everyone seemed to change the subject. It was very strange considering Nero, Vincent, and Amo had been inseparable their entire lives, yet now she never saw him around.

Getting up from the huge couch, not about to let anyone change her mind, she walked right up to the huge giant. "Hey, Amo."

"Hey." He didn't even bother to look up from pouring himself a drink.

A coldness came over her, just from looking at him. She hadn't seen it until she had gotten up close. He wasn't the Amo she remembered. There were dark circles under his eyes, and a certain presence around him that hadn't been there before. A presence that was very dark and even more haunting.

She started to regret coming over to see him, now understanding why everyone had changed the subject when she had brought him up.

"I-I haven't seen you in a while."

"I've been busy."

When he finally looked at her, she wished he hadn't. It took only one look to know that the Amo she had once known ... was dead and gone.

What happened to him?

"Hello." Angel came over to stand beside her.

Thanking God, he had come over to save her. She started to introduce him, "Amo, this is Ange—"

"I know who he is." Amo's dead voice matched the deadly stare he gave the Luciano.

Angel didn't take his eyes off him, returning the deadly stare.

"Adalyn, I think Lake needs you. She was asking for you."

Swallowing hard, she nodded, knowing Lake hadn't really asked for her

It felt wrong when she left Angel with Amo. There was clearly history between the two. What that was ... she was too scared to ask.

Angel had come to this party for one reason and one reason only. All night, he had searched the eyes of every Caruso to find the man he was looking for, and now he was standing right in front of him.

The two stared each other down in silence, waiting for the other to speak while their eyes communicated their visible hatred.

His eyes didn't waver from the dead ones he would remember for as long as he lived. *This was for Drago.*

"I know who you are." Angel's low voice came out like a cruel whisper.

Amo took the smallest step toward him, trying to intimidate him with his height alone. "Is that supposed to scare me?"

"It should." Angel stood his ground, unafraid of Amo's size. Angel was quite a few years older than him. He knew he was merely looking at a boy who had just become a man. The reason he knew that was because he, too, used to have that look in his eyes, back when he didn't know the type of man he wanted to be or where he belonged. "Do you see Joey here? I'll save you the time of looking around and tell you that he's not. I've seen many Carusos come in and out of here all night to wish your consigliere a happy birthday, but I haven't seen him. How about the third guy? Do you see him? I don't know who he was, but I'm guessing you haven't seen him in a while either."

Amo kept his mouth shut, not saying a word.

"What do you think Lucca did with them?" As he smiled, an evil twist curved his lips. They both knew the games Lucca liked to play. "How much longer do you think you have before one of them breaks and tells him? What do you think the boogieman will do to you then?"

Amo squared his jaw; finally, there was a flash of something that wasn't just dead behind his eyes. "Why don't you tell him?"

"I wanted you for myself." Angel looked him straight in the eyes, seeing the thin strand of fear he tried to hide. "But I've changed my mind. I'll let Lucca have you."

Amo took another step toward him, his chest almost touching Angel's now as he gave his own threat. "You are and always will be just a pawn in a dangerous game of chess. You're a piece on a board to Lucca, just like me. And when he's through with you, he'll only keep you around for his sick, fucked-up entertainment."

"He did something to you, didn't he, Amo?" Angel maintained the evil smile, knowing that whatever punishment Lucca had brought him was better than anything he himself could do, and the longer Angel waited for Lucca to come for Amo, the better. "Know that when the boogieman finally does come for you, it wasn't me who told him he lost control of one his youngest, weakest men." As he walked away, an evil laugh escaped. "He'll find that out for himself."

"You're doing exactly what he wants," Amo warned.

Angel stopped, turning back around to face him. "What did you just say?"

"He's always five steps ahead of you, and he knows every move you're going to make before you even make them, because it's exactly the move he wanted you to make. He wants you here, and he wants you with *her*." Amo's gaze moved over to Adalyn, who was across the room. "She's a distraction to keep you here willingly." His dead eyes moved back to him. "You didn't think he'd actually let you go, did you?"

Angel looked at Adalyn, then at the demon who was more capable and clever than anyone he knew.

"You're slowly becoming less of a Luciano every day that you're here, but I promise you this … you will *never* become a Caruso. You'll just be nothing."

"Nothing? Like you?" he asked, seeing the empty shell of a man. "You're lost, Amo. You lost to him. But there's a difference between us. I. Don't. Lose." *Ever.*

Those dead eyes gave him one final promise from experience. "Lucca always wins."

A MATCH MADE FROM HEAVEN AND HELL

Taking an empty seat beside Chloe, Adalyn didn't move her chocolate eyes away from Angel, watching their quiet exchange from afar. When their exchange ended with Amo finally leaving out the front door he had just come in, she took a deep breath and turned to the scarred beauty.

Chloe had followed her eyes, seeing Angel for the first time tonight. Goose bumps visibly rose on her pale skin.

"He scares you ..." Adalyn whispered unknowingly. Never had she been able to talk to Chloe about the horrible things that had happened to her at the hands of Lucifer, and never had it been any of her business. Seeing her look that way at Angel, completely terrified, it did start to involve her.

I need to know if I'm making a mistake.

Pale, haunted gray eyes looked away from the fallen Angel to her.

"D-did he do something to you?" Adalyn asked nervously.

Chloe started to wring her hands.

"I'm sorry. I shouldn't have asked you that." She bit her lip, regret settling in. Taking another deep breath, she admitted something that frightened her. "I only asked because … I think I like him … a lot."

Chloe stopped fidgeting, now only lightly squeezing her hands together. She could see it, the truth about how Adalyn felt about Angel.

Taking her own deep breath, she focused on her words. "When L-Lu …" Pausing, she couldn't get the devil's name passed her lips. "When h-he took me, Angel and his twin circled me the entire time." Chloe's voice dropped to an almost whisper, like she was fully realizing something for the very first time. "I-I think they were protecting me."

Adalyn looked at the tatted bad boy, a smile forming at her lips. Knowing about Matthias and thinking about how each brother had circled her as well, she fully believed they had been protecting Chloe that night.

"It's just …" Gray eyes looked back at Angel, the fear still apparent. "They look just like *him.*"

Goose bumps now trickled on Adalyn's tanned skin.

"I-if they didn't look so much younger, didn't have all those tattoos … I would th-think I was looking right at the devil."

Adalyn's eyes travelled down the length of Chloe's scar, sending a shiver so deep it rattled her bones. *I'm so sorry, Chloe.*

"Come outside with me, darlin'," a low voice appeared with an outstretched hand.

Watching the broken girl take the demon's hand sent a pain to her heart and continued to do so as she they walked out the back door and into the gazebo, where they sat. Without thought, Adalyn had gotten up from the couch, finding herself staring out one of the many windows, just to gaze at them a little longer.

Too enthralled, she hadn't even noticed Angel standing beside her until his voice haunted her. "You really love him, don't you?"

Her instinct was to lie, but she couldn't find it in herself to do so. "Is it bad that I want to be her? That I want a love like that?"

"Yes, it is." The response was harsh and took her off guard. "Their love is twisted, almost sick." Putting a finger on the glass, he pointed at the couple. "I want you to look at them, Adalyn. Really look at them. Individually, they are fucked up in their own ways and need the other to survive. They are doomed apart. God help them if one were to endure life longer than the other. Their love is the rarest of all. A sick one that's only made beautiful by those two souls and those two souls alone."

The scarred beauty and the boogieman, *a match made from heaven and hell.*

"Is that really the *love* you want? Is *he* really the man you want?" Angel took her chin in his hand, forcing her to look up at him. "I know things about the boogieman that wouldn't only give you nightmares in your sleep, Adalyn, but every time you opened your eyes."

Looking into the eyes of the son of Lucifer, she could feel her heart splitting in two. "I don't know what I want anymore."

Angel dropped his cold, tatted fingers from her face. "I can tell you now, sweetness, it's not going to be me."

Her vision blurred.

"Goodbye, Adalyn."

MY WEAKEST CREATION

"You *wanted to speak to* me?" Lucca asked, sitting back in his chair.

Angel looked at the city that was backdropped behind him, not speaking for several minutes, letting everything that had happened since coming here sink in. When he finally spoke, he looked the demon right in the eyes.

"How long are you going to keep me here, Lucca?"

"When I no longer have to worry about your family coming after mine, I will let you go, and not a moment sooner."

Shaking his head, realization settled in. "As long as both our families exist, there will always be that possibility, Lucca."

The underboss put a cigarette to his lips and lit the end with a quick flick of his wrist. "Then you better get comfortable."

You didn't think he'd actually let you go, did you?

That mocking voice rang through his ear as his blood began to boil. He could see it. The cage he was trapped in was being locked and the key was being thrown away … and there was nothing he could do about it.

Getting up, he needed to get away from him before he did something he would undoubtedly regret.

When he placed his hand on the doorknob, the voice came back. *He wants you here, and he wants you with her.*

Angel had already made the decision where she was concerned, but it was time to write it in stone.

Turning around, his low voice echoed in the room. "I am no longer capable of watching Adalyn. I want a different position. It doesn't matter to me what it is as long as I never have to see her again."

"Is that really what you want?" Smoke blew from his mouth with each word he spoke.

Nodding, he knew it was time for him to stay a step ahead of the boogieman.

"Fine." Lucca got up, coming to stand in front of him. His blue-green eyes narrowed on him as he inhaled deeply on the stick. "Do you know why I picked you, Angel? Why, out of all the Lucianos, I picked you?"

It was a question he had asked himself every day. A question he was finally about to get the answer to.

"I thought you were different, smarter, stronger. I thought you brought more to the table than the rest of them. I knew you were the only one who could handle it, and now"—Lucca narrowed his eyes on him even more—"I'm not so sure if you're going to make it."

Angel could only stand there, watching him retake his seat behind the desk.

"I wanted the kid I saw that day at the train tracks, but I don't see him anymore when I look at you. Prove me wrong, Angel, or you might as well jump out of your bedroom window."

Opening the door, Angel had heard enough.

As he headed back to his hotel room, it seemed like every wall started to close in around him. Therefore, when he made it to the safety of his room, he went straight to the dark closet, closing the door on himself.

The dark, small space surrounded him as he placed his hands on the closet wall, closing his eyes...

...As the sound of the train in the distance got closer, he looked down at his feet. They were inside the metal train track.

He looked over at his sixteen-year-old twin brother, who stood right beside him.

"If you fucking move before I tell you to, you get the closet for five days," Lucifer yelled at them from a few feet away. "But if you're the first to move, you get it for four."

The light of the train could now be seen as it barreled closer and closer, brightening the night sky surrounding them.

Angel looked over to see Matthias close, his eyes to the light.

"A Luciano fears nothing!" Lucifer's corrupt voice matched the ferocity of the train heading toward them.

The light from the train now touched their skins, as the train's horn began blaring for them to move out of the way.

"Not a train, not a bullet, not a man, not the darkness. We fear nothing!" the devil continued to yell, not giving the command to move.

Sliding his feet into position, he was ready to run first, not from fear, but from the thought of his brother not lasting four days in the closet alone.

The evil voice boomed the word, "Go!"

Angel took off, moving from the train tracks, only hoping he was the one to run first, but when he looked behind him, Matthias was still standing there with his eyes closed as the horn blared in their ears even louder.

It didn't even take him a second to see that peaceful look on his brother's face to know his brother had no plans of leaving that train track. The sweet release of death was the only thing that could save them from their father, and Matthias wanted it.

The power in which Angel took off, running toward his brother, shook the ground. Fear was something his father had made sure he didn't have, but it wasn't until he thought of his life without his brother that he realized he was capable of it.

The train speeding right at Matthias wasn't going to reach him first, because that wasn't an option. He was either going to save his brother, or they both were going to die the same way they had come into this world. Together.

As he ran straight into him, their whole lives flashed before his eyes in a single moment as he wrapped his arms around his brother and jumped.

When the force of the rushing wind passed them, he almost thought Matthias had gotten what he wanted, until he realized no pain or suffering had greeted them. Still, he held on to his brother tightly, not letting him go for several minutes while the long train passed.

The look on his brother's face before he had saved him, a look he hadn't seen on him for years, finally thinking he had found peace … But Angel had taken it away from him; therefore not saving him after all.

A hand on the back of his shirt pulled Angel off Matthias, and then he was forced to face his father.

Lucifer's fist met his face with such a force that it sent Angel flying to the ground. Spitting on his fallen body, he then lifted his foot, bringing it down on his neck to choke his son. "You don't deserve to bear the family name."

Angel brought his hands to his father's shoe, trying to release some pressure to breathe.

"Unlike you, Matthias is strong . . . waiting to jump until the very last second." He dug his shoe in a little deeper. "You're my weakest creation yet."

Choking, he felt his life force begin to leave him.

"I'll make a man out of you, or you'll die trying." Releasing his foot off his neck after digging harder, he spat on him one last time. "Seven days you get in the closet when you make it home."

Angel breathed heavily, letting the air fill his lungs once again while he lay there on the gravel, watching his brother being helped up by their father before they walked away.

The blood that trickled into his eye blurred his vision as darkness started to sweep him away after losing too much air. It was only right before it claimed him that he heard footsteps come toward him and a pair of blue-green eyes stared down at him when everything . . . just . . . disappeared . . .

THE FIRST FOUR STAGES OF GOODBYE

Walking *outside into the cold* air the next day, Adalyn felt sick. Not until the Escalade pulled up and no Angel could be found did she realize her fear had come true.

All night she had been in denial, crying and promising herself that not until he didn't show the next morning would she believe that Angel had said his final goodbye.

Goodbye, Adalyn.

Now she knew with finality he had.

Before Adalyn's knuckles could meet the door, it was flung open and Lucca appeared, letting her inside his office.

As he took a seat behind the desk, she decided to stand, too anxious to sit. It had been a week since Angel had told her goodbye and disappeared. Even the hotel room he had stayed in was empty of him.

"Where is he?" she asked, getting right to it. She was angry at herself for asking, but even angrier that he would disappear the way he had without even giving her a chance to speak.

Lucca leaned back in his chair. "I can't tell you that, Adalyn."

"Why?" She almost screamed the word, knowing it was wrong to be so angry, but it was inexplicable.

He was silent for a few moments before he told her the truth. "He told me he doesn't want to see or speak to you."

When the tears finally fell, they changed her vision. For the first time, she saw the man she had been in love with, with different eyes, realizing she hadn't actually been in love with him at all. She had been infatuated with him, with the idea of him, of loving the underboss, of loving the boogieman.

How did she finally know that after all this time? Because right up to this moment, she hadn't felt what it felt like to really, truly love someone.

This time when Lucca spoke, there was a slight tenderness to his voice. "I'm sorry, Adalyn."

Wiping away her tears, she looked at him, not knowing if he was sorry for Angel disappearing out of her life or for making *me fall in love with Angel.*

Sitting on her bed, she couldn't keep from looking out of the corner of her eye at the ring that sat on her nightstand. It had haunted her every day for a month now, as it was the only thing she had left of him. The only thing that let her know it had all been real and not just a dream.

Adalyn picked up the horse shoe ring, twirling it between her fingers. She had hoped, even expected, that he would come back into her life, even for just a moment, to get the ring back. She had been keeping it, planning on using it to bargain with him when he did, but he hadn't. And that only made the hurt so much worse, considering it was so important to him. It showed her that he would rather she keep it until the end of time than to see her again.

It was so cruel and so hurtful that it shattered every part of her to the point where she didn't know if she could ever trust herself to love again.

There were some wounds that cut deep, but others just killed you.

"How much do you love me?" Adalyn gripped the ring that she had hidden in her jacket pocket.

Lake eyed her warily as they sat at the counter, pretending to be interested in their homework. "Depends on what you want me to do. If you want to copy my homework, I love you enough to share it. But if you want me to do something that's going to get me in trouble with Vincent, it's debatable."

"Wow, that hurts. So, you're picking my brother over me again? I thought it was chicks before dicks?"

"Adalyn!" her friend grumbled, knowing it was hard for her to say no when she pulled that card. "I can't get in trouble with Vincent right now. He finally loves me again."

"When's the last time we got in trouble? We never have any fun anymore …" Adalyn's voice trailed off, too depressed to continue.

"Uh … Are you trying to make me feel guilty?"

Looking over at her, there was at last, after one month and one week, hope in her eyes. "Is it working?"

"Goddammit." Lake shut her book with a hard *thud*. "How much trouble am I about to get into?"

Adalyn smiled, hoping there was still some adventure left in Lake. "The kind where we steal Vincent's keys and get the hell out of here."

Regret was already written on her best friend's face. "Well, fuck me."

Standing up, Adalyn was more than ready, having thought about him enough. The first four stages of goodbye were hard; it was time for her to meet the last one.

AND THE LAST

When the neighborhoods changed from carefully maintained ones to ones that became unkempt and old, she wondered if this really had been a good idea. By the time Lake slowed the car to a crawl, she didn't think it was.

"Adalyn ..."

But she wasn't going to let her friend know that, because her mind had been made up the second she had put the ring in her pocket.

"I'm going to do it, Lake. What's the worst that could happen?"

"An axe murderer could open the door." Her friend paused for a moment. "Or she could be prettier than you."

She had told Lake on the way about Angel, about the ring, and the name she had been given that had put a sparkle in his eyes.

Swallowing painfully, she unbuckled her seatbelt. Then the nerves really started to hit her as she got out of the car. *I would rather it be an axe murderer who opens the door.*

Giving Lake a determined glance, Adalyn walked up to the porch of the tiny old house and opened the squeaky screen door to knock on the main door. She tried not to be so scared by the bars that were covering the windows, but it was easier said than done.

When no one answered, she tried one last time, knocking harder.

Hearing the door unlock several times, she backed up, preparing for the person behind it. But when the door was finally opened, revealing a beautiful young woman, her breath was almost knocked out of her.

"Hello?" The beautiful woman seemed frazzled.

"H-hi." Nervous, Adalyn tried to catch her breath. "Are you Bella?"

She seemed to be a bit nervous herself, especially that Adalyn knew her name. "Yes. Who's asking?"

"Um, my na—" When smoke started to pour out from behind Bella, she watched as the woman quickly left her.

Not knowing what to do, hearing frantic groaning coming from inside the house, she decided to go inside to see if Bella needed help.

When she walked in, her eyes scanned the tiny home that was meticulously clean and neat. She could even see the vacuum trails on the carpet that went in the same direction. The throw pillows on the couch were so evenly spaced apart that Adalyn wondered if she had used a ruler.

It was easy to find the path to the small kitchen that was consumed by smoke. Waving it away from her face, she saw Bella opening the kitchen window to release the heavy air, then pulling out a burnt casserole dish from the oven.

Watching Bella bow her head in frustration, she thought about how this was going very differently than she had thought it would. And the longer she stared at the woman, the more her heart dropped.

She could see why Angel had had that look in his eye when he had said her name. Her name did her justice because no man would be able to resist the exquisite beauty of this dainty woman. Her natural, dirty blonde curls tumbled to her shoulders with a glossy shine that perfectly matched her strong, dark brows. She was without a doubt gorgeous, not needing a stitch of makeup or fancy clothes to prove it.

Adalyn pulled the ring out of her pocket, giving it one last squeeze before heading toward to the frustrated beauty who seemed to be at the end of her rope.

"I think this is yours."

She stared down at the ring; tears began to brim the blonde's eyes as she took it, clenching it in a tight fist. "Where did you get this?"

Adalyn tried to open her mouth, but she couldn't. She couldn't find it within herself to get the words out.

Tears started to fall onto Bella's high cheekbones. "It's my father's ring …"

That right there was exactly why Angel had tried so damn hard to get it for her, and now she finally understood everything.

If Lucca had been the one with the ring, the chances of her father being dead were certain. The ring, which was the last piece she had to remember Angel, was now Bella's last piece to remember her father.

Life was funny that way, or twisted and fucked up, depending on how you looked at it.

Bella wiped at the tears. "Please tell me where you found it. I have to know."

Looking at the beautiful woman for one more second, she wondered if she knew she had her very own guardian angel. An angel she would have killed to have.

"I'm sorry. I can't." Adalyn backed up before running straight for the door and to the car. She was strong, but she wasn't strong enough to keep looking at the girl who had stolen Angel's heart long before she had even had a chance in hell.

With each mile Lake drove in silence, Adalyn felt her heart lighten more and more. The first four stages of goodbye were over, and the last had finally washed over her.

Acceptance. It was a ten-letter word that stood in front of you before you were finally ... set free.

As she looked over at her friend, for the first time in a while, a smile appeared on her lips. "Can we make one last stop?"

"Of course." Lake smiled back. "Where do you want to go?"

Smiling even wider, she could practically taste the nuggets already. "McDonalds."

The door was flung open as he approached.

"Angel!"

Catching Bella when she jumped into his arms, he wrapped them around her, lifting her off the ground and holding her to him. For a split-second, he forgot everything as he smelled her blonde curls and the sweet vanilla scent that clung to them. He held her a little longer. It only ever lasted for just a moment . . .

. . . "Angel!" Bella gave him a big hug when he walked into school.

Wrapping his scrawny arms around her, he smiled, knowing that, even at eight years old, this moment right here was what would make living through his father's hell worth it for the years to come.

"I missed you so much," she whispered to him.

The horror he had spent in the closet seemed to all slip away. "I missed you, t—"

"Matthias . . .?" The little, curly blonde girl let him go, slowly walking up to the identical brother with sadness marking her face. "Are you okay?"

Matthias blankly stared, seeming to look straight past her. His dark gray eyes were traumatized, and if you looked close enough, you could see the horrors he held in them.

With water glistening her young eyes, Bella raised a hand, reaching out for the brother she would always reach out to for years to come. "Matthias?" . . .

. . .Holding out for a second longer, he felt Bella's gaze go over his shoulder and sensed the disappointment that her gentle nature couldn't hide.

See? Only ever lasted for just a moment.

Placing her back on the ground, he took a deep breath and let her go. "It's just me. Mathias couldn't get away."

Her smile slightly faltered. "Oh ..."

He hadn't seen her in what seemed like forever, being trapped in that casino hotel room. Miserable from not being able to see her, he had asked Matthias to switch places with him again for just a few hours. Coming back to her now seemed different.

Reaching up, he smoothed his tattooed knuckles down her cheekbone like he usually did when he saw the sadness appear on her face. Every time he did, without fail, he wished it could soothe her the way it did when Matthias did it, wished he could soothe her the way Matthias did when she saw him. Never had he been able to achieve his goal, and not until this moment did he realize it was never going to be achieved.

Bella was and always would be in love with Matthias, regardless that he had shown her little interest. No matter how identical they were on the outside, they didn't share the same soul, and Matthias was who her soul called to.

Only made beautiful by those two souls and those two souls alone ... He remembered the words he had said to Adalyn the last time he had seen her, making him realize that he was just as blind. Angel hadn't taken his own advice.

Trailing his knuckles across her skin for a second longer, he knew this would be the very last time he would do so. The joy and love he had felt for her while touching her was now gone. He wasn't meant for her, and he could finally clearly see she wasn't meant for him.

As he started to remove his hand, he stopped, seeing a ring dangling down from a chain around her neck. Angel trailed his hand down, picking it up. He recognized it immediately.

"Where did you get this?" he asked, rubbing it between his fingers, making sure it was real and not just a mirage.

"A girl came to me about a month ago." Taking it from his hand, she stared down at it. "She didn't tell me her name or where she found it, but when she gave it to me, it felt like she had been keeping it safe. And when I took it ... she seemed upset."

Angel gazed down at the ring that was now being twirled in Bella's hand, a ring he had tried desperately to get back to her.

When he had walked out of Adalyn's life, he had still wanted to get it back, but if he had seen the pretty brunette again, he wasn't so sure he would have been able to walk away from her a second time.

Ultimately, deep down, he supposed he knew why he couldn't see her again, but it wasn't until right now that he could admit it to himself. *I'll be trapped forever.*

It was time for Angel to make a decision, one that could change the course of his life forever. And once he made that decision, there was no going back.

Looking down at the girl he had been in love with his entire life, he said something he should have said over two months ago.

"Goodbye, Bella."

When *Adalyn left her house* Monday morning, the black car was already waiting for her. She opened the car door and got into the back seat when her heart came to a complete stop.

She had spent one month crying and the second one getting over the man who now sat in the driver's seat as if nothing had ever happened.

No. No. No.

She jumped back out of the car, slammed the door, and started running back inside the house.

Angel quickly got out and ran after her.

"Adalyn!"

"Leave me alone!" she barked at him.

"Please." Reaching out, he lightly touched her arm, stopping her. "I just want to talk."

Adalyn gazed down at the tatted hand on her arm while tears

started to rim her eyes as she remembered how, with every passing day that had passed, she could remember less and less where each colored ink lay on his pale skin. It only caused her to wish and wonder what it would be like to see him again, to feel him again.

But she wasn't that girl anymore.

Pulling her arm away from his grasp, with tear-filled, defiant eyes, she looked straight into his gray ones. "I wanted to talk months ago, but you wouldn't let me."

"I couldn't," he told her truthfully before opening his eyes, letting her see what he was hiding, even to himself. He whispered the words; there was no hiding anymore. "I'm scared shitless, Adalyn."

She stood there, paralyzed, listening to every word.

"I'm trapped here without knowing if he will ever let me leave. If I allow myself to have you, I'm afraid I will stay forever."

A single tear trailed down her face. "Then why walk back into my life?"

"I don't belong here, sweetness. We both know that." Angel stepped closer to her, wanting to reach out and brush away her tears. "But I think I might belong with you."

"Why now? What changed?" she quietly asked.

He had to do it.

Reaching out with a cold, inked finger, he wrapped a strand of her thick brown hair around it. "I realized I could either spend an eternity here, *trapped,* or I could spend an eternity here, *with you.*"

As she stared up at the fallen Angel, she realized that the love she felt for him hadn't gone away. Instead, she could feel it growing with every passing second. It was so tempting just to reach out ...

He's going to break you again, a small voice whispered, reminding her that she had moved on and had accepted things the way they were. If she gave Angel another chance, he would leave her when Lucca released him. She didn't think she could survive it.

Adalyn pulled the strand from his grasp, watching it unravel from around his long finger. "You already walked away from me once, Angel. Now, this is me walking away from you."

She proudly walked up the porch and opened her front door.

"I know you gave her the ring back. I want to thank you." His voice stopped her from going in just yet. "I thought I was in love with her, but she's always been in love with someone else. Does that remind you of anyone?"

Squeezing the door handle, she didn't want to turn back and look at him, afraid she would lose her composure.

"I'm telling you right now, any love I had for Bella is gone, and I'm willing to look past any love you might still have for Lucca." Angel tried one last time to get her to take him back. "You didn't deserve what I did to you, and for that, I'm sorry, Adalyn. It's no excuse, but I'm fucked up. It's how I've survived. I can't promise you much of anything because of that, but I'm willing to try to make you happy, if you'll let me."

She looked back at him as more tears streamed down her face. *This time, I need promises.*

Shaking her head, she made up her mind. "I don't think I could ever trust you again."

Angel gave her the only promise he could while watching her close the door on him. "I can wait. I'm not going anywhere, sweetness."

Tuesday morning, after calling Lucca and telling him that she wouldn't go to school with Angel, she was taken off guard to find both the Escalade and a black car parked outside.

Seeing Angel waiting as he leaned against the hood of the car, and then looking at the Escalade that held all her friends, she realized she was being given a choice.

Adalyn took a breath and walked down the driveway. She came up to Angel's car first but didn't even turn her head as she walked right past him, not even the slightest bit tempted. It was almost like he didn't exist.

When Wednesday came, she was met with the same two choices. Still, she found the choice easy. *Escalade.*

Thursday, Angel was still there. She was starting to get a bit annoyed, which made it the tiniest bit harder to walk past him again.

Her eyes drifted as she passed, glancing at the bad boy before she snapped them forward. *Still Escalade.*

When Friday rolled around, she found her resolve starting to slip. Thinking it would only get easier to pass him, she found the opposite was the truth; it only got harder. She promised herself she wouldn't look at him, but again, her eyes slightly drifted. However, that wasn't the worst part. This time, something else happened within her.

She felt her skin cry out for his; the missing pieces they had stolen from each other with each encounter were still there. It felt like a tether that was impossible to walk away from, but somehow, she did and got into the big SUV. *Thank you, God.*

A MAN WHO WAS MADE

After *the weekend, she felt* refreshed when she opened the door on Monday morning. There was no way he would still—

Why?!

Biting her lip hard, she started the journey down the driveway, beginning to pray. *Dear God, please give me the strength to walk past this unbelievably arrogant man.* She repeated the prayer over and over in her head and, with only one little glance, she was able to walk past a still patiently waiting Angel.

The Escalade door was opened, and Maria stepped out of the back seat to allow her to squeeze in. She couldn't help noticing the strange look Maria gave her as she got in and climbed into the third row between Elle and Lake.

The tall blonde paused for a moment before she finally got back in, closing the door behind her. She sighed as the car started to pull away, then Maria's voice filled the confined space. "Wait."

They all looked at her when the car suddenly came to stop.

"Everyone out," the mafia princess commanded, and she was instantly obeyed as the doors flew open and they all started to exit. When Adalyn started to leave, Maria pushed her back. "Not you. You stay."

What the—

Her eyes grew wide when her butt immediately fell onto the seat beside her.

Vincent didn't want to shut the door, clearly assuming what she was going to talk about. But when Maria gave him a threatening glare, he slammed the door shut.

In the now private space, the princess stared her down. "What the hell are you doing?"

"Well, I was going to schoo—"

"I meant, what the hell are you doing riding in here?" she hissed. "I can't watch you turn him down anymore."

To say Adalyn was stunned by the words coming out of the princess's mouth would be an understatement. Never in a million years would she have thought Maria could care about something that involved a Luciano enough to meddle; yet she could tell by looking into her eyes that, deep down, for some reason she did.

Trying to keep her voice strong, she told the blonde, "He left me, Maria."

"Well …" The blonde raised a brow. "He's here now, isn't he?"

"Yes … but he hurt me. How am I supposed to trust him again?"

Maria's fierce gaze bore into hers. "He's been here every day for the past week, and even though you continue to turn him down, he keeps coming back. Open your eyes and look at him. If you think he's going to give up, you're wrong, Adalyn. Men like Angel never lose," she promised her, her eyes growing more captivating the longer she spoke. "If you can't find it within yourself to trust him, then I was wrong about the type of man you were looking for, because I thought you wanted a man who was Made."

"I do," she whispered.

"Out of all the Lucianos, Lucca picked him. There's a reason he did that; you just have to be brave enough to find out what that reason is."

Swallowing down the lump rising in her throat, Adalyn admitted the real reason she didn't want to take him back. Every Made man always needed one thing. "I'm afraid ... he'll break me."

Maria reached over, lifting her chin high with long, manicured fingernails. Enunciating each word that passed her lips with an intensity like no other, she told Adalyn, "Then. Don't. Let. Him."

Angel got back into his car after being turned down yet again. He had come every day, wishing she would give him one more chance, but she hadn't. *At least not yet.*

Having nothing but time, he would come back every single day if he had to, to get her to trust him again. As far as he was concerned, their little game wasn't over, and he had plans on winning.

His eyes went to the rearview mirror, seeing all the doors to the Escalade open and then everyone getting out—*almost* everyone. He held his breath as a ray of hope shined down upon him.

Come on, Adalyn. He squeezed his tatted knuckles around the steering wheel so hard it was beginning to imprint the leather.

Still holding his breath, he stared a hole into the mirror as he watched the doors open once more. But when they all got back inside and the doors closed behind them, the hope he had for her forgiving him today vanished.

Angel put his hand on the key that sat in the ignition, ready to turn it, when his eyes were drawn back to the rearview mirror.

A slow smile started to twist up his lips.

Having said her piece, Maria snapped her fingers, giving the others the go-ahead to file back into the car.

It was all up to her now.

Adalyn avoided the gazes of her friends and her brother, unable to look them in the eyes as they got in the car and shut the doors. When she heard the car start up again, she felt her heart starting to race and pound out of her chest. She found herself more torn than ever, the temptation stronger than ever. Still, she didn't move to get out of the car.

I thought you wanted a man who was Made.

Those words swirled through her mind, reminding her that

was exactly what she'd wanted and prayed for in a man, yet she was walking away from one. A real one.

Upset, she guessed a part of her had wanted him to apologize repeatedly and beg her to forgive him, but that wasn't who Angel was. He had said the word "sorry" already, and he wasn't going to ever beg. You either forgave him or you didn't. And him coming here every morning was his way of proving to her that he had meant what he said. She could either take him for what he was, or she could continue to walk away, but the choice was hers.

She put her hand on the door handle and flung the door open, making a decision she could one day live to regret with only one thing for certain ... It would be one hell of a ride.

Vincent wasn't happy, calling out in his sharp voice, "What are yo—"

"Don't you dare," Maria cut him off. "I'm sure Lake will take him if you don't want your sister to have him."

His baby blues slightly flamed at her before he sat back, giving in.

Lake and Elle's muffled clapping and cheering could be heard from inside the car as Adalyn closed the door behind her. Then she walked toward the black car, but when the driver's side door was opened, revealing a smiling Angel, her feet picked up speed until she was running. Then she took a leap of faith and jumped into his arms.

It was the moment she had been waiting for when he circled his arms around her and held her to him.

For some odd reason, even though her blood bled for the Carusos and his Luciano, it just felt right.

A few tears slipped down her cheeks as she nestled into his neck. "If you leave me like that again, I'll kill you."

Angel laughed. "Is that a threat, sweetness?"

"No." Kissing his neck, she smiled. "It's a promise."

After he placed her back on the ground, he used his thumb to wipe away the tears from her face before he grabbed her chin, tilting it up for him to stake his claim on her.

By the time he touched his lips to hers, her mouth was already open for him, but as much as she wanted to kiss him back, she didn't. She wanted him to be the one to kiss her so she could see how much he actually wanted her.

This kiss was different than the rest he had given her. The same passion, the same dominance, but she could also taste something new.

Need.

Adalyn kissed him back, then, with the same need showing through her kiss as a moan passed her lips and into his warm mouth.

When he pulled away, his voice came out in a low growl when he ordered, "Get in the car."

"Why?" she asked, dazed, not knowing if she had heard him right.

"Because if I don't take you to school right now, you're not going."

The intense gray eyes she stared up at showed her what kind of need he was feeling. She gulped loudly, having about three point five seconds to get in the car before her virginity was gone forever.

"Now," he growled, giving her one last warning.

Adalyn wasn't stupid . . . She ran to the passenger door.

God, I'm not sure if marriage is going to be for me.

BAD BOY DREAMS COME TRUE

A dalyn held his hand tightly, smiling as they walked to the car. "Do you get a winter break, too, or is Lucca going to make you work?"

He squeezed his tatted hand around hers. "I'm not sure. He hasn't told me anything yet."

"What?" Vincent stopped in his tracks, causing Lake, who was walking under his arm, to stop. "He already told me I have casino surveillance."

"Hmm … I'm sure he just hasn't told me yet." Angel gave him a slick smile.

The pretty boy thought for a second before he continued, "Yeah, you're probably right."

Adalyn quietly chuckled, happy that it had been Angel to steal her heart. It would have been really hard to have a love life with her brother around, but Angel was clever, knowing exactly how to handle him.

She was happier than ever. Finished with her first semester of college, surrounded by her friends and family, and having her bad boy dreams come true.

They had been together for some time now, taking it slow and making sure the Caruso family adjusted to the possibility of the two families mingling. It had been an uphill battle, but they were sure Lucca had put the fear of God in all his men. She also figured that was how Vincent had quickly adjusted to Angel.

Walking up to the Escalade, she saw the tall, gorgeous blonde who was standing next to Elle give a smile as they approached. "Hey, lovebirds."

Or maybe that was Maria.

"Hey, princess." Unlike everyone else, Angel wasn't afraid of her and could dish it right back. There seemed to be an understanding between the two. Even Adalyn wasn't sure what that was, but she knew it had to do with a mutual respect.

When they heard rolling wheels spinning on pavement, coming right at them, they all turned their heads.

Uh-oh . . .

"What the . . .?" Elle's mouth dropped open, and Lake froze like a statue as Matthias rolled over to them on his skateboard, stopping to stand right beside Angel, his complete mirror image.

"I missed you, brother."

"What the hell are you doing here?" Angel asked.

Matthias's eyes travelled to a pretty, young girl who passed them.

"Well, I came by to see what kind of gig you had here, and now I would like to volunteer to take your place."

"Too bad." Angel wrapped his arm tightly around Adalyn. She thought he was holding her awfully close …

"Wait!" Elle's eyes bounced back and forth. "What?"

Lake's eyes rolled to the back of her head as she passed out, her body going limp.

Adalyn went to catch her, but Vincent already had, screaming in frustration, "What the fuck!"

"I take it she didn't know you had a twin either?" Matthias asked, looking down at the fallen girl.

"Jesus Christ," Maria muttered, rolling her eyes when Elle and Adalyn started fanning Lake. "You girls need to keep your shit together."

"Well, hello …" Matthias finally noticed Maria, trailing his eyes down her body as he rolled his skateboard toward her. "I haven't seen you in a while. You're looking good, princess."

Maria picked up her stiletto-donned foot, stopping the board from coming any closer. "Don't even try it." It was clear by the glare in her eyes that the respect she had for Angel didn't transfer to his twin, or any other Luciano for that matter.

"Just let me know if you change your mind, princess." Matthias gave her a sinister smile as he backed up, able to take a hint.

Lake had started to come to, but she passed out again after she heard Matthias talk that way.

"Fuck this shit." Vincent picked her up and threw her over his shoulder. Grumbling under his breath, he went to place her in the car. "Now she knows there's fucking two of them prettier than me."

Adalyn couldn't help laughing at her brother, who had desperately tried to keep that little secret from his girlfriend.

"You should probably go while you have the chance," Angel told his brother.

Matthias agreed, but before he took off on his skateboard, he gave Maria another one, "See you around, princess."

The blonde narrowed her eyes at him as he sailed away. Looking to Angel, she gave him a message. "He better hope not."

Understanding, Angel nodded as he took Adalyn's hand again, leading her to the car.

"You two are complete opposites, aren't you?" she asked when they were alone.

"In every way but appearance."

Looking over at him, she felt it starting to click. "Is that why all your tattoos are flipped, because you are opposites?"

"No." His voice took on a dark tone as he revealed the real reason they mirrored each other. "My father made us do that so he could tell us apart."

Every hair on her body stood up. It was the first time he had spoken about his father to her. After hearing about who he was and what he had done to Chloe, that alone had made her sure she never wanted to hear more.

"Oh."

When his response was silence, she figured he didn't want to tell her more about it.

Angel continued to walk her to the car, where he opened the door for her, but she didn't want to get in just yet. Needing to spend a little more time with him before he took her home, she reached up on her tippy toes and placed a hard kiss on his lips.

He grabbed the small Italian girl's tiny waist, holding her in place. "What was that for, sweetness?"

"I just thought I'd give you a kiss, so you'd know what you'll be missing over winter break."

"So, you don't want to keep seeing me?" he asked with a smile.

"Oh, I do. That was in case you didn't want to see me." She leaned up and wrapped her arms around his neck, keeping him there for just a bit longer. "Where are we supposed to hang out every day now?"

Angel was the one to place a rough kiss on her lips this time. "Get in, sweetness. I've got something to show you."

No *fucking way …" Adalyn breathed* as she stepped into the empty penthouse apartment. It was bare, with no furniture, and much smaller than the other ones she had seen on the top floor, but the view was damn sure amazing. "How did you …? When did you …?"

"Lucca gave me the keys last night and said it was mine if I wanted it," Angel told her.

She looked over at him, noticing the devoid expression on his face. The happiness she initially felt started to drift away, replaced with sadness. "You don't want it?"

"It's not that I don't want it. It's what it means if I take it."

She darted her tongue out to lick her lip, nervous for what he was about to say.

Angel stalked toward her, then began to walk around her in a circle. "The fact that he even offered it to me tells me he doesn't plan on me leaving." His gray eyes moved over her body. "And if I take it, that would mean I accept the fact that I will be trapped here ..."

She breathed heavily, and her heart began beating faster and faster the more he stalked around her.

He stopped right in front of her, bringing a single tatted finger to the base of her chin, slowly tilting her head higher and higher. Then he said the word that held one final guarantee, "Forever."

The beating in her chest grew louder.

"Do you know what forever for me means for you, sweetness?"

She held her breath.

"An eternity with me." He said the words with such a force that they seemed to shake the room.

She heard the strong pounding in her chest ringing in her ears.

"Is that what you want, sweetness?" He pressed his fingertip into her chin even more. "Because if not, you better walk out of this room right now."

Her eyes drifted to the door, knowing this was going to be her last chance.

Sliding them back across the room, she then looked him straight in the eyes, telling him exactly what she wanted. "I want you."

Angel grabbed her neck, pulling her lightly toward him, letting her see him for all that he was. "You sure about that?"

He was everything she ever wanted, and then some.

"Absolutely."

Bringing her to him, he gripped her tighter, sealing it with a kiss.

Not expecting what was to come next, she found her feet being swept off the ground as Angel carried her up the steps to the lofted bedroom. It all happened so fast, and not until she was tossed onto a mattress that had been placed in the middle of floor did reality return.

Looking at the bed that was covered in white sheets and pillows, she propped herself up on her elbows and looked up at him in confusion. "I thought he gave you the keys last night?"

Angel's fierce eyes moved over her approvingly. "He did."

"But …?" *And if I take it, that would mean I accept the fact that I will be trapped here … forever.*

"I accepted it the second he handed me the keys." He bent his knees, falling onto the bed, then moving his body to cover hers. "I'd be trapped with or without you, sweetness."

Her breath caught in her throat as he inched his face down to hers, stealing a quick kiss. Then another.

Each kiss he stole became longer, more passionate as he stole her heart along with it.

He pressed his body down on hers harder, making her fall completely back, as he became more demanding with his mouth. She wasn't afraid of his hunger. In fact, she matched his intensity with her own needs, pressing her breasts harder against him as she rubbed her tongue along his, darting it into his mouth to tempt him further.

She moved her hands to his waist, slipping them under his T-shirt and exploring the muscled flesh beneath. She had never touched a man's body before. She found it invigorating, her own body tingling from the sensation of feeling his cold flesh.

A low growl escaped his throat, telling her she needed to proceed with caution, but Adalyn had waited long enough. She was still in need from the time he hadn't given her a release that night in the elevator.

Moving lower, she slipped her fingertips into the waistband of his jeans.

Any constraint he had left in him fled.

He swiftly removed her sweater and thin bra before going to her waistband and pulling down her jeans and panties in one swoop with the lift of her hips.

With her fully exposed to him, the flash of need shining through his dark gray depths made them lighter. They travelled from her dainty face down to her small, round breasts, to her tiny waist and small hips. "Goddamn, you're gorgeous."

A rush of heat flooded her cheeks.

Not wanting to be alone in her nudity, she looked up at him through heavy lashes and said, "Let me see you."

When Angel removed his shirt, exposing every inked inch of him, her eyes widened. It was a glorious sight.

Reaching up, she couldn't resist running her fingertips over the tattoos, tracing them, wanting to commit each one to memory. She started at his chest, then went down to his lean abs, and then even lower to where she saw them dip inside his jeans.

"How can one person be so perfect?" she whispered to herself, unable to stop tracing them.

"I'm not perfect, sweetness." Angel stopped her hands as he leaned down, darting his tongue out to quickly lick a taut nipple.

"I'm far from it."

She had practically moaned when his warm tongue touched her. Grabbing his shoulders, she dug her nails into his skin, wanting and needing him to continue. By the time he took her breast into his mouth, sucking the sensitive area, she was almost ready to come.

When she wrapped a leg around his waist and pulled him closer to her, her exposed pussy raked against his jeans, and she felt his hard length that was so close yet so far away.

He unbuttoned his jeans, setting himself free in an instant. His need was too much for him to handle anymore.

Holding himself above her, he placed the tip of his shaft at her opening and gave a small thrust to notch inside her without warning.

The cold reality of what she was doing rushed over her as Angel entered her, moving slowly through her channel, invading where no one had gone before. The stark truth was, with each thrust, the more deeply and madly in love with him she became. She wanted Angel. She liked the way he felt against her; the tingling, electric currents that went through her at every thrust that only kept growing in intensity.

At first, he moved slowly and gently. Then, as he drove deeper inside her, he started moving faster and harder, rocking his hips against her while placing featherlight kisses along her jawline. It was a sensation she had never experienced. The intimacy was like nothing she had never imagined. And that it was with a Luciano made it even more irresistible.

She buried her face in his shoulder to muffle the sounds she was making as he moved inside her. Each stroke sent ripples throughout her as she wrapped both legs around his waist and began moving back against him.

Her nails must have been digging into his skin too painfully because he jerked them away and held them pinned to the top of the mattress above her head.

Angel was controlling not only his but her movements now as he increased the passionate intensity between them. She could only go where he led her. And where he led her was a magical place right between Heaven and Hell. With Adalyn taking him to Heaven with each deep thrust into her pure, untainted body, and Angel taking her straight to Hell as he came inside her, claiming her and tainting her as forever his.

The son of the devil and the Italian beauty.

She had finally found her own version of love that she had desperately craved. *My own match made in Heaven and Hell.*

THE NIGHTMARES
HE HAD ENDURED

Waking up in the middle of the night, Adalyn felt the bed beside her, finding it empty. "Angel?" Her voice echoed in the vacant space.

When no reply came, she sat up, trying to open her eyes and see through the darkness. She didn't find him anywhere upstairs.

As memories of him leaving her haunted her, she got out of bed and went down the steps. She walked through the apartment, finding it empty.

Please, God, not again. Her heart stopped, knowing it had all been too good to be true.

Adalyn paced the empty floors of the house, hoping and praying it wasn't what she thought, trying to stop herself from jumping to conclusions. That was when she heard heavy breathing coming from a closet. She stopped in her tracks.

She walked to the door and turned the knob, holding her breath for what she would see behind it. What she found tore her heart in two.

A sleeping Angel on the cold, hard floor. Tears flooded her chocolate depths.

"Angel," she softly whispered, not wanting to scare him awake as she bent down and placed a hand on his arm.

He jumped awake the moment she touched him, and she quickly pulled her hand back.

The second he realized it was her, the fight in his gray eyes calmed.

Adalyn immediately regretted waking him up instead of just going back upstairs and pretending she hadn't caught him sleeping in a closet. It didn't seem like something he would want to talk about, let alone for her to know.

"I'm sorry." She went to leave him, but he reached out and stopped her.

Not saying a word, Angel pulled her into the confined space, making her sit down then laying his head in her lap.

Her heart somehow broke a little more as she stared down at him while trailing her fingers through his hair. She didn't expect him to give her an explanation; nor did she need one. The dark circles under his eyes and the nightmares she could see in his gray depths told her all she needed to know for now.

The longer she sat there, running her fingers through his hair, the more she realized he might never tell her why, and that was okay with her. For a man as proud as Angel to let her see this meant he must really care about her. Knowing that few people on this earth, if any, knew this secret, she was content.

Very few times in a person's life there were moments sincerely precious, and this was one of hers.

Out of all the Lucianos, Lucca picked him.

Whatever Angel had gone through, she could now feel exactly how much of a survivor he really was, and she felt honored to be in his presence.

Continuing to smooth her fingers over him as he fell back asleep, she thought about the day that might be years and years down the road, when he would tell her about the nightmares he had endured.

"I can wait. I'm not going anywhere, Angel."

A MONSTER HAD CREATED HIM

He thought the *returning memories* would get better after being with Adalyn, but they hadn't. She helped soothe them, but they always somehow managed to come back, taking him in the middle of the night.

Staring at the demon behind the desk, it was time Angel moved on. *And I've come to do exactly that.*

"I know he's alive."

Lucca's blue-green eyes glowed. "Who?"

"You know precisely who," he said, wanting him to cut the shit. "If I know the boogieman, which I think I do, then I know you've kept him breathing."

"What is it you want, Angel?" Lucca asked, not denying anything.

An evil smile appeared on his lips. "I want you to take me to see him."

The blindfold was taken off his face after he had been led into an old, damp building at an unknown location. He looked around, seeing a huge, metal sliding door in front of him. He walked up to it and placed his hand on the cold metal. He could feel what he wanted behind the door.

Before he could open it, Lucca warned, "If you so much as think about fucking killing him, everything I did to him ... I'll do to you."

I don't doubt it.

Gripping the handle, he slid the heavy door open, and with every inch it moved, light poured into the dark room until it reached the back wall, highlighting the frail body that was curled up in the corner.

Angel stepped into the room, moving toward it, when the bright fluorescent lights were turned on, lighting the space with intensity before the door was slammed shut behind him.

The frail man covered his eyes, protecting them from the bright lights, while he quickly rose up the dingy wall behind him. It looked like he was cowering away from the intruder, but then his eyes finally adjusted, and he blinked several times before he realized who it was, and a maniac laugh escaped his throat.

"Matthias, is that you?"

Looking down at him, Angel noticed every mark that marred his father's naked, filthy body. Every single one of them hadn't existed on his pristine pale skin prior to his current situation. If he didn't know any better, he would have thought twenty years had passed since he had last seen him. That was how much he appeared to have aged.

His eyes travelled from his scarred head down his mangled body, and then to the chain that shackled his ankle to a pipe in the corner.

Angel took another step toward the man who had made twenty-three years of his life a living hell. "Hello, Father."

Lucifer sat back when he saw Angel move more into the light, his hopeful expression gone. "Oh, it's you."

"I've always known how to disappoint you, haven't I?"

"Without fail," Lucifer hissed.

Walking over, Angel sat down on the filthy ground beside his father, placing his own back against the wall. He got the full view his father would enjoy for the rest of his days.

"Why did you come here? To gloat?"

"Before coming here, I thought you actually might have begged me to release you." Turning his head, he stared into evil, black eyes. "But I realize now that was stupid."

"I'm a Luciano. We don't beg," Lucifer practically spat.

No, we don't, Angel agreed.

Sitting in the cold silence, he finally asked the question he couldn't before. "What is it that makes you hate me so much?"

"All my sons brought something to the table, except you." Lucifer's brows came together, trying to find the word. "You're neutral."

Confused, he asked, "Neutral?"

"My sons either wanted to be me ... or feared me." Lucifer was proud to say that his lips twisted up with a smile, but then they quickly turned down. "You didn't have either in you. Therefore, you were worthless to me."

He knew his father had lied about how a Luciano shouldn't fear a single thing when all he wanted was to instill fear in not only his men but his own children. The fear Lucifer had craved most was fear of him.

"Matthias, though . . ." Crazed laughter bounced off the walls. "I remember when I broke him. He snapped so easily. Even like this, I bet I could scare him into releasing me."

Having heard enough shit spew from Satan's mouth, Angel got up, the temptation to kill him too strong.

"He needs me! My children need me! The family name will not continue without me because the family's nothing without me!" The chain around his ankle rattled as he tried to stop Angel from leaving, grabbing the bottom of Angel's leg to get the metal object he knew he kept there.

Angel stopped him, placing his shoe on his father's hand.

"You're wrong, Lucifer." Using all his weight, he pressed harder, hearing bones begin to snap. "We're stronger without you, and I'll do everything in my power to make sure you fucking live long enough to see it." Releasing his hand, he began to walk away as Lucifer's fanatic laughter sounded again, echoing repeatedly.

"I did you a disservice, keeping you in that closet for all that time. It made you lazy and complacent. That closet was the only space you deserved, and it's all you'll ever deserve."

Angel reached out, flipping the switch to kill the lights. Darkness enveloped him, his father, and the very room they were in. The only noise to be heard was the softest, quietest rattle of the chains around Lucifer's chest as it rose and fell.

Closing his eyes, Angel could almost taste the cherry flavoring of the candy he had come to love.

As he listened carefully, the rattling softly grew louder as Lucifer's breathing picked up speed, rising and falling at a different pace.

"A Luciano fears nothing," Angel whispered. "Not a train, not a bullet, not a man, not even ..."

The rattling grew.

"... the darkness."

Opening his eyes, he slid open the door, letting light pour into the room for only a few more seconds. Then Angel walked away from what he hoped would be the last time he would ever see that face, a face that scarily resembled his, reminding him every time he looked in the mirror that a monster had created him. A face and body he and his twin brother marred with tattoos, desperate to cover up that very fact. Each tattoo they had inked into their pale skin had made it easier and easier for them to look in the mirror, until they could finally face their reflections without destroying a mirror. It could drive even the strongest man insane when every time you looked at yourself, you didn't see you but someone else, someone who had abused and tortured you your entire existence.

And out of the two of them ... *one had.*

Angel placed his hand on the door, getting one last good look, with one final thing to say.

"It's ironic to think you trained me for the exact place you are in now. I would outlast you in there, you know. I lasted twenty-three years in my hell and didn't break once. That's why you hate me so fucking much. You just can't admit it." Smiling, Angel started to slide the door closed, letting the darkness have him. "Just know, it's a hell of a lot bigger than the closet you kept me in. Tell me, Lucifer; how long are *you* going last?"

Slamming the door shut felt therapeutic, freeing, like he had finally closed a book on his life and was ready to start a new one.

"How was it?" Lucca's haunting voice sounded from behind him.

Angel thought for a moment. "Better than I thought it ever could be."

"Good."

Angel turned around, his gray depths staring into the demon's eyes. "I'm going to need something else from you."

Lucca stared him down with evil eyes, waiting.

"You don't get to kill him … till every one of my brothers get to have him."

THE FINAL GOODBYE

Looking *down at the city,* she continuously tapped her heels against the hard floors.

"He's waiting outside," Lucca told her as he stopped beside her.

She had always loved this spot right here, where she was fully able to see what could have been hers.

"Maria ..." he tried to get her attention.

Hearing the muffled screaming, she snapped her eyes to her brother. "Does he know what's waiting for him?"

"I thought we could surprise him."

She looked out the window again, her eyes roaming the many buildings, entranced as Lucca stood beside her, seeing exactly what belonged to him and not to her. Maria quite enjoyed doing this with her brother, finding it relaxing. She supposed he did, too, by the number of hours they spent doing it while they talked.

Hearing the muffling, fervent praying, she was drawn out of her thoughts again.

"So, brother"—looking to Lucca, she got back to the business at hand—"have you figured out who the one-shot killer is?"

He seemed to be annoyed as the words passed his lips. "He hasn't revealed himself to me yet."

"And what is the boogieman going to do with Amo?" she asked with a smirk plastered on her perfect face, dying to get an answer for this one last question.

A demonic pair of blue-green eyes almost lit up the room. "I was hoping you had something in mind."

The screaming got louder now, making her tap her stilettos again.

"We can come back to that."

Maria went up to the window and pressed a button on the wall that slowly slid the shades over them. "Send him in."

"Come in," Lucca commanded the person on the other side of the door.

Turning around, she watched the door begin to open as the screams grew in intensity.

Opening the door, Angel took in the room, seeing Lucca and Maria standing behind a man tied to a chair. The sight didn't change his expression.

He walked in and closed the door behind him, then stepped onto the plastic that was spread out on the floor underneath the chair. He stared right at the man who was tied and gagged. "He's mine?"

Lucca nodded.

It was always easy to spot the fear in a man's eyes, especially before the final goodbye. The man he now looked at tried to find that same fear in Angel's eyes, but sadly, he came up short.

Leaning down, Angel pulled out the metal object he kept hidden under his pant leg. Flipping it open with the flick of his wrist, he twirled the butterfly knife in the air. It spun so fast it blurred to the point where you could no longer make out which part exactly was the handle or the blade, until it slashed the crying man's neck.

"Goodbye, Joey."

AN ETERNITY LIKE THIS

When the door was opened, Adalyn ran, jumping into his arms and wrapping herself around him.

Angel caught her and held her to him. "What are you doing here, sweetness?"

"I got you a present." She placed a kiss on his lips before she jumped back down and took his hand, leading him upstairs.

She was a bit nervous to show him, hoping she hadn't overstepped. *God, please let him love it.*

Angel stopped suddenly once he had reached the top of the stairs.

"D-do you like it?"

Walking up to the queen-sized canopy bed, Angel moved the black curtains that draped over the rods. Then he turned his head to look at her before he held out an inked hand. "Come here."

She walked over to him, placing her hand in his.

When he continued to stare down at her for several moments, she felt the need to explain herself, quickly rambling out of nervousness, "I thought it might help you sleep. When you close the curtai—"

Angel captured her lips with his, giving her a kiss she would never forget.

Slightly dazed, she smiled up at him. "So, you do like it?"

"That depends, sweetness."

Before she could finish asking "On what?" she found herself quickly turned, the top of her meeting the soft mattress as she was bent over the bed.

Sliding her thick hair away from her face, he bent over, covering her body with his, to whisper in her ear, "On how you look on it."

Her eyes practically rolled to the back of her head, feeling the heat begin to burn inside her from his words. She didn't think he moved fast enough when he quickly pulled down the top of her jeans and released his hard cock to tease her opening. Adalyn wiggled her ass back, making him shove his shaft deep inside her.

Forced to scream into the sheets by the position he held her locked in, she got louder and louder with each pounding into her.

The place where he took her was always so beautiful ... but this time when he took her to between Heaven and Hell, it felt different. More special somehow.

Moaning out her sweet release, she didn't think spending an eternity like this was so bad.

I love you, Angel, Adalyn said in her head, too frightened to say it out loud in case he had changed his mind on forever.

Adalyn reached up in the darkness to run her fingertip over the four dotted diamonds under his eye. "You haven't told me yet if this tattoo has a meaning."

"Each dot represents a Luciano brother." Angel started to trace a diamond on her back with a tatted finger, starting with the top. "The top one is for my oldest brother, Dominic. The two on the sides are me and Matthias. And the bottom one is for my youngest brother, Cassius."

Laying her head on his chest, she snuggled into him. "Do you have any sisters?"

He went quiet for a few minutes, thinking about his words carefully. "Yes."

"Do you not want to talk about it?" she asked politely.

"Not yet, but soon, sweetness," Angel promised.

She placed a kiss on his chest, able to accept that. "Okay."

Smiling into the small, dark space they shared under the canopy, he wasn't sure what he had done to deserve a girl like her. Maybe it was the suffering he had gone through. If that was the case, *it was worth it.*

Angel leaned down, breathing in her thick brown hair that smelled of cherries. He hadn't realized she smelled of cherries until he had come back to her after two months. The second she had run into his arms, he had smelled that sweet cherry scent, making him wonder how the hell he had missed that in the times he had spent with her.

He supposed it had to do with Bella. She had clouded his vision of Adalyn. The second he had told her goodbye, though, he had finally been able to see Adalyn for the beautiful, caring, and fiercely loyal woman she was. She had told him several times now that he made her dreams come true, yet she had sent his nightmares away. *Forever.*

A vision of a new book slowly opening appeared in his mind. It was time he started a new beginning.

"Adalyn …" He placed a long, inked finger under her chin, making her look up at him. "I love you."

OUTLAST

I am trapped by the walls that hold me.
Trapped by the mind that fools me.
Trapped by the bones that keep me here.
But I must not give up,
For I must win,
To see your face,
When you realize,
That I will
Never
Ever
Give in

Sarah Brianne

Please, if you or someone you know ever needs help,
follow this link to get more information and help.
YOU ARE NOT ALONE.

www.victimsofcrime.org/help-for-crime-victims
/national-hotlines-and-helpful-links

Made in the USA
Las Vegas, NV
28 February 2021